BELOW

ALARIC CABILING

CONTENTS

PART 1

THE FIRST WAVE: TONDO, MANILA, PHILIPPINES

(Site of the First Zombie Apocalypse)

CHAPTER 1

DEATH AND DESTRUCTION, 2022

Barangay Happyland was home, and it was in flames. It was one of the poorest districts in Tondo, Manila, where the largest, most congested slums were found in the Philippines, as well as the world. Minutes ago, the zombies had broken out of hiding. First, from drug addicts that mysteriously changed. Next, from victims who had been bitten. They ran riot like a termite swarm buzzing around a fluorescent bulb, attracted to flesh and blood, not light. They multiplied, feeding like voracious eaters. After infected cases started increasing in the shanties where we lived, they spread like wildfire. Literally. Fires burned down homes. Bodies fell into the stagnant tarn. The polluted bay filled with corpses. It was Armageddon.

Collisions stopped traffic on intersections. Desperate drivers jammed the streets. It wasn't long before the roads were unusable, and cars lined up for miles. Overturned trucks crowded highways; panicked motorists left their vehicles behind...and never returned home.

There I was, one of the few survivors, a mere child, wondering what to do. Victims were screaming, zombies bobbing over them, feeding on their living tissue. Their sausage-link sets of intestines were hoisted in the air in a gruesome feast. Their hearts were ripped from their chests. Their choice meats—liver, spleen, pancreas—were eviscerated.

Fire was devouring any unusable substance. The toxic fumes suffocated.

One zombie passed through my area, eyes alert, hunting for strays, for children who were small, who were hiding in the tightest spaces. The zombie gnashed its teeth, hissed. It breathed hard like a predator on the prowl. I hid beneath a table, yet I could hear.

The zombie went down the hallway between neighboring homes, hungry for its next meal. It looked so much like Mama, like Mama used to be.

In the not-so-distant past, there had been Mama and Papa, my only family, serving me meals. I worked as a scavenger in the landfill, making very little money, enough for cheap canned meat and some rice. I never complained of eating too little, or getting too used to the same food. In the zombie apocalypse, there were few provisions. You had to break into people's houses to steal what supplies you could find and escape the zombies that would come your way. They came out at night. If you were lucky, you would be back someplace safe until morning. Someplace remote. Like the sewers.

Life in Tondo before the zombie apocalypse was hard enough. You were a slave to the grind, the worst way how—scavenging for recyclable wastes, going knee-deep in refuse.

———— ◆ ————

From underneath one table I darted to a fence, climbed over it, felt the wire hot to the touch, scalding. My hands came away with burns. I couldn't stop. I had to keep going.

Over to my left, there were more zombies; to my right, the coast was clear. Easy decision to make. I dashed to the right and hid behind a trash bin, finding a group of scavengers-turned-zombies feeding on a middle-aged woman nearby. Too late to save her. They took big bites into her flesh, tearing away at muscle and layers of fat. She screamed. I could only look away, barely able to tolerate her cries.

I broke out into a run. I crossed an open area, seeing zombies feeding on another woman on the ground. I recognized one of the zombies. My stomach sank. I was aghast. It was my friend…feeding on another victim, nearly all night. I was scared to meet him head on, face him, no room to get away. What would I do then?

I recalled scavenging in the landfills with him. I remembered being new, when I was determined to help my mama and papa put food on the table.

———— ◦ ————

Poverty was one thing; a catastrophe was another. When friends died brutal deaths in the zombie outbreak, the sinking feeling worsened. Grief swept over me like a tsunami. I would stop, breathe, relax, and cry silently so no zombie would hear.

That became increasingly hard to do. In congested Tondo, the zombies were everywhere. One bite was all it took to turn one healthy adult into a blood-crazed, flesh-starved maniac. Something would happen with their blood vessels, looking like they were carrying some kind of poison. Their muscles would stretch taut; their skin would change texture; their gums would darken. Neither animal nor man, but instead monster, a newly awakened zombie was deprived of compassion, immune to its rapidly disintegrating memories of love. I had seen it in the eyes of my transformed loved ones. Whatever good moments you'd shared were gone. Simple. Don't expect mercy from a zombie.

Before the apocalypse broke, Mama and Papa had warned me. "The isolated incidents are growing more common. The police and military are having trouble containing the contagion. A bite brings irreversible symptoms. What else do we do but hope and pray?"

Indeed, in the Philippines, the indigent person placed faith in miracles. A stroke of luck was greeted with devotion. An empty pocket brought desperation—drugs. Drugs signified more than rebellion. Drug use enabled sweet oblivion. To forget about hardship, forget about obligation. As far as I was concerned, I had never wanted to run away from my situation, to forget or deny. There was a way to refuse the corrupt establishment, to resist the force of gravity that kept poor, uneducated peoples stuck in the mud. It didn't involve drugs, a prayer pamphlet, a lotto ticket. It involved education. I knew early on. Literacy was my way out of poverty. I read books and enjoyed them, treasured them more than my real circumstances.

I read YA adventure books like *Choose Your Own Adventure* and *Wizards, Warriors, and You*. I had fun reading. I saw so many things I couldn't find in Tondo's shanties. Entire worlds formed out of my imagination. They gave me hope. Hope meant everything.

⸺ ⬦ ⸺

Months earlier…

In Happyland, drudging the mire allowed for survival. No one was immune. Not to the stench. Nor the ridicule. To outsiders, we lived in intolerable conditions, but we were used to it. Better to scavenge the landfills for material wastes to resell than beg for alms on the street. In fact, kids in Barangay Happyland didn't beg. The streets were muddy, the landfills toxic.

Such is life in the slums of Manila, and Tondo contained some of the city's worst slums. The shanties were built beside the highly polluted water of Manila Bay. The primitive dwellings were stacked on top of each other like floors in a building, neither by concrete nor stable footing. Hallways snaked in and out like labyrinth tunnels; in these tunnels, doors opened into small, ramshackle rooms.

Trash littered the muddy trenches, sacks full of rubbish lined the roads and adjacent homes. Here, capitalism reared its ugly head in a polluted landscape. Mass consumption fed the poorest of the poor.

In the slums of Barangay Happyland, garbage settled on roadsides in mountains, where people would not tell the difference. People did not mind the stench. They were used to it. What choice did the homeless have?

In the polluted bay where we dumped sewage from our homes, no light could penetrate, no amount of cleaning could ever fix.

On my first day scavenging, I asked the junkshop buyer how much I would get for my recyclable wastes.

"Eighty pesos per kilo of plastic wastes; five pesos for copper wire," he said.

I thanked him. "How's business?"

"We're always open. There's always garbage."

Scavengers made less than six dollars on most days. The occasional gold-nugget find made them ecstatic. There were too many unemployed, impoverished citizens living in sub-human conditions in tight, congested quarters.

This is where the city threw their waste. These landfills were sorted, and the scavenged goods sold back to recyclers. The remaining trash often entered the bay area or stayed in mounds on the roadsides in Happyland. The waters were black as oil, murky as charcoal. Fish floated on the water, unable to breathe due to bacterial saturation.

I lived in such a slum. My name is Luzvimindo Arnaiz, Min for short. The name Luzvimindo stood for Luzon, Visayas, and Mindanao—the three main island groups comprising the Philippines. I was twelve years old. My family and I lived in a squatting community of hundreds within a small land area—a part of Barangay 105 in Tondo, Manila, the place famously known as Barangay Happyland for its smiling, playing children.

The landfills were located within walking distance. Dump trucks stopped at roadside. Residents used jeepneys and tricycles for public transportation. Private vehicles consisted of motorcycles.

When I returned home from classes after 3 p.m., I scavenged at our landfills for glass bottles, aluminum foils, cartons, and cans to help with our bills. I carried a big, black garbage bag over my shoulder and back, and used a stick to prod the mountains of refuse.

There were flies everywhere, wings buzzing on fat, blue-black bodies over piles of food waste and ripe juices. Dogs and cats were on every street, feeding just like flies.

Coming home from the landfill, I would typically find my mama waving from the second-floor window of our shanty, smiling and calling me. "Min, I brought food for you and your papa." I would run up the stairs.

Papa would already be inside, eating. He was a quiet man who worked construction jobs for most of the week, coming home on the weekends after sleeping at the construction sites. While he spent most of his time on construction sites, he never smoked or drank. I would walk inside and hug him at the table, then get seated so I could eat.

Mama worked full-time at a canteen serving customers meals, often tying her hair in a ponytail to prevent it from getting in the cooking. She was very gentle. Mama couldn't yell at anyone nor harm a fly.

Drudging the mire in Tondo was life. Wading in refuse and heat was everyday reality. Together with Papa—Josel—and Mama—Frances—we tried our best to weather life's challenges.

But poverty was only the beginning of our plight.

The years digging for gold in the dirt of Tondo's landfills came back to haunt me, when salvation was harder to find by hazard than a worthwhile book in the public library. Unlike a large hunk of metal to sell to a junkshop dealer, which equated to good money, enough for a number of meals, YA books offered a glimpse into another world that money couldn't buy.

Every day, old and young alike hunted for gold in the trash in Barangay Happyland. All the items recycling plants didn't want stayed in our back yards. Most residents scoured all day long. We waded in trash as it poured out of the dump truck and hurried to find any steel or pricier valuables.

The smoke rising from the garbage heaps looked like spirits on Halloween, like dry ice inside a funhouse at a carnival. I prodded the waste materials with a stick and placed them into my bag with my bare hands. Sometimes, I wiped my nose and forehead with my dirty hand or arm, causing me to get sick with a variety of conditions. My mama said, "It's natural. Where else would we find a means to make a living?"

In overpopulated, polluted Metro Manila, that just seemed to be the case. Landfills were a cheap source of employment. Else you begged on the streets, working for syndicates.

It seemed like trips to the free clinic came as often as my trips to the produce and meat stores. However, besides sickness, Mama told me about kids that violated curfew, prompting policemen to detain them. "Conditions are abominable in youth detention centers, where smaller kids are beaten or raped by the bigger ones. The centers are tight, caged spaces packed with many kids. Be careful that you do not end up in places like those."

I was an obedient child who never strayed too far from Happyland. There was too much work to do, too little money.

We had family photos in our little house close to the bay. And although we were poor, we weren't miserable. We had genuine smiles on our faces in the photos.

The trouble started close to home.

Home consisted of two adjacent rooms. First, a living room with a window that looked out into the bay—a space where we slept and ate our meals. The next was an open kitchen space where the sink was located.

Beside our unit were several others stacked together like a tiny apartment building. We were located on the second level. Papa had helped build our home, and explained the construction once. "I used wooden clapboards and old signs for some of the walls, while the roof consisted of discarded yero, steel sheets that I nailed to wooden beams and weighted down by rubber tires."

In the neighboring units, families huddled; sometimes, solitary rooms were inhabited by single residents who worked jobs in construction or as security guards for stores, banks, or malls, while some worked as meat and produce vendors to residents in the community. They set up stores all over Barangay Happyland, smiling at residents like me.

Now imagine all that dilapidation. Imagine our primitive wooden housings being subject to electrical sparks from broken lamps. Imagine the fires raging, the communities of people hiding from the zombies having no choice but to leap to their deaths into the polluted bay, where they would be anchored down by the trash on the ocean floor to drown. Imagine these homes with fragile locks on their doors, easily broken down and entered. Imagine me making my way through one corridor to another, seeing if friends of my father's had survived, and finding none. There were bodies, barely recognizable.

Imagine dodging one zombie trying to get a bite from your neck. Imagine adrenaline spurring your tired legs in an all-out run for the walls and fences. Imagine climbing rusty barbed wire and incurring cuts. Imagine pulling away from the grasps of zombies' outstretched hands—a warzone.

Imagine firetrucks waging a losing war to kill the fires, the firefighters under attack by the zombies. Imagine the massive inferno, smoke filling the sky. More survivors were turned to zombies. More burning bodies fell into the polluted water, the screams echoing.

So many neighbors ran amok as fully transitioned zombies down the hallways. The inhuman screams were deafening. The sound of flesh flayed from bone by dull teeth was excruciating to bear. The sound of blood sputtering from a hard bite turned my stomach.

The trouble really started in other neighborhoods, with teens in other homes close to Barangay Happyland who did drugs.

Older kids who resided in other districts across the Radial Road R-10 who used drugs to cope with poverty didn't influence me. My parents had warned me explicitly.

"Min, promise you will never turn to drugs to drown your troubles," Mama asked me one night. "Promise?"

I nodded and gave my word.

I continued to read my textbooks.

In those shanties, teens who attempted to numb the pain brought by lifetimes of abuse and hardship did drugs and started to look and behave like zombies. They turned to the most primitive means to seek temporary relief. Cheap methamphetamine: a drug called *shabu* by locals. Afterward, they opportunistically stole, picked pockets, snatched cellphones and handbags, and worked as runners for drug dealers to get their stash.

But then, they changed; they grew hungrier, more savage.

They looked gaunt, emaciated. Their limbs twitched and spasmed. Their eyes widened in anticipation of drugs...or food.

The reasons behind the transformation were a mystery. No one had seen it before. Drugs deteriorating people's brain functions, reducing them to starving, hunting wild animals. Isolated cases popped up, and the police contained them. But when the outbreak ensued, the infected cases were overwhelming.

All that time, in the district of Happyland where I lived, we thought we were safe. Yet, it was crowded, congested there. An outbreak of horrific proportions was going to be easily catastrophic, with victims piled high as the assailants went on a smorgasbord. Cutting through the shanties, on benches outside stores, or deep within rooms untouched by the sun, addicts took more drugs and transformed daily, multiplying in number, amassing into an army.

The next battleground was school.

We found drug addicts there, and they, too, were transforming...

CHAPTER 2

THE SEWER

Back in the present, Tondo was burning and I was certain that the rest of the country was too. I thought hard about a place to go. Moving from one hiding place to another was paramount. There had to be a safe haven, a refuge from all the killing. But where?

I got on my motorcycle and crossed the other side of Barangay Happyland in search of someplace safe, passing buildings where bodies fell out of third-floor and second-floor windows. They bounced off the ground spasming and shaking, transforming. They came roaring at me. I raced ahead, squeezing into tight spaces between abandoned cars on the road, sometimes twisting away from the grasps of zombies inside the cars.

Weaving through stranded traffic on bloody streets with my motorbike made me edgy. My eyes homed in on any sign of movement, any chance of getting bushwhacked, whether by a zombie hiding somewhere, or by the confused police and military, who were gunning down residents indiscrimantly. Riding without a helmet or protective clothing, the uneven roads caused my bike to jump clumsily, making me nervous. I did my best to stay in control, grappling hold of the handles despite my sweaty hands. With the wind gusts thrashing my t-shirt and hair, the inferno on both sides of the road radiated warmth.

Somewhere out there, I had to believe that the military or police were rescuing people, despite seeing them shoot everyone in sight, zombie or not. It was an eradication. Genocide.

The only place I could think of to seek help…school. The evacuation centers were similarly taken over by zombies. I passed one on C.M. Recto Avenue and witnessed a slaughter, a holocaust.

While zombies tore through the streets, I made the decision to hide at Amado V. Hernandez Elementary School. The school was empty, the gate swinging open by the rusty hinges, making that ominous sound, like steel grating steel. It was night when I happened by campus, peering inside to see whether school teachers had made it out alive and were seeking refuge. One look at the open gate and the opaque windows of the classrooms and I knew. Would I venture inside and dare hide in a cramped, dirty janitor's closet? Would I hide in a locker too small for me to move my limbs?

Students had been home during the outbreak of violence. It was a weekend, which explained for the school being dark and empty. Who knew if zombie students or zombie janitors lurked within, waiting in the darkest classrooms on campus, maybe the restrooms, looking if survivors would sit in the bathroom stalls—an obvious *no-no* because survivors would have had no escape.

Yet, in the face of all the challenges finding a suitable hiding place in Tondo, Amado V. Hernandez Elementary School would offer one place I would revisit later.

Weeks before…

The school was a long walk from home but worth it. We didn't waste our precious savings on tricycle fares. We crossed the overpass on the Radial Road R-10 to the other side of Barangay Happyland, the better section of the district.

The walls of our campus were decorated with bright, colorful murals. Mango trees stood over the waiting sheds. A security guard stood by the gate, ushering students inside after inspecting our bags.

My friend, Bodjie, and I attended the same school. He lived in a room under the Vitas Bridge with his parents and three siblings, and was the biggest kid in our *barkada,* our friendship circle. He was the joker, the teaser. Bodjie scavenged with me during nights and weekends. His dad worked in a repair shop, while his mom sold goods in a little store.

It was the first day of school again, before the zombie apocalypse would break out.

There were many students on the grounds, laughing and talking.

I made a new friend. His name was Jason. He was, by our standards, much better off, but his dad could no longer afford private school tuition. Most of the middle- and upper-class residents of Manila put their kids in private Catholic schools. Jason used to attend Don Bosco School in Tondo before transferring to ours. His first day must have been hard; knowing no one, being new to a public school and everything. Private schools in the Philippines were almost certainly always better, different from the United States and Western countries. Still, teachers told us that we could achieve anything we set our minds to. We could make the most of our education and get ahead in life.

When class started, I said hi to everyone in my gang: Bodjie, Laleng, and Enrico. Enrico was a laid-back guy who lived in Barangay 101, also by the bay, next to Barangay Happyland. He was wiry thin; his hair was split in the middle, with long bangs upfront. If Bodjie was the joker, then Enrico loved to play *contrabida,* the villain, because he tended to be sarcastic. We would jeer at him.

Laleng was a skinny girl with pigtails, although she sometimes wore braids. She lived in Barangay 103, which was the closest to school in our group. Laleng had smooth, brown skin. She was not mestiza, not fair-complexioned like some well-off girls, but she never complained about being *kayumanggi*, brown-skinned. We lightly made fun of her for being so bravely patriotic and sensible. "*Magsalita ka*, Laleng. Say something. Come on! Bleach! Bleach!"

When Jason and I went to the restrooms during recess, he recited a jingle, then made his monster face and lit it with his flashlight.

Jack en poy
Hale, hale hoy
Sino matalo, siyang unggoy!

I told him the word "unggoy" meant "monkey," and not "monster."

His monster face suited him though. After we peed, we headed to carpentry class.

<hr />

Basic carpentry had its own area on campus. There were jigsaws, handsaws, drills, hammers, large working tables and benches. Jason, Bodjie, and I sat at one workbench and listened to Mr. Sevilla teach in front of class.

After Mr. Sevilla was done explaining our first project, he sat behind the teacher's table and let us work. Jason, Bodjie, and I got to telling stories while sanding our wood board.

"So, Bodjie, where do we head after school?"

"I know a place. A big construction site next door. Nice place to play hide-and-seek. Want to smoke there? We can do that too."

"What, Bodjie? Smoking again? You're much too young."

"That's because you're a baby, Min. Why don't we just play hide-and-seek instead?"

I glanced over at Jason, and he gave us a puzzled look, so I gave

Jason a nudge. "That's okay, Jason. Join us. We'll invite the others: Laleng and Enrico."

"Okay, guys. I'll come," Jason answered.

We officially had one more member of our little gang. I smiled at Jason and slapped him on the shoulder. We worked in quiet for some time, focusing on our project.

The rest of the day passed quickly, one class after another getting lost in the shuffle. Only notes in our notebooks to tie together the various echoing words and sparse memories of study chapters and syllabi. Jason, Bodjie, and I rounded up Enrico and Laleng to join our little misadventure after dismissal time at 3:30 p.m. We were glad to get through the first day of sixth grade, and we strapped on our backpacks and trotted down the street outside campus to the nearby construction site. It was deserted. They had stopped construction temporarily after the school briefly suspended face-to-face classes.

The property was closed off by a makeshift gate made of rusty steel sheets, walled off by a perimeter of broken concrete with holes big enough for kids to get through. We found one hole and parted the long stalks of grass that posed as hindrance. We entered the gap, crunching empty soda cans and plastic bags under our shoes. On the other side of the wall, the lot had a big gaping hole in the middle—a foundation, maybe. Drainage ports made of large, hollow, cylindrical concrete blocks were scattered around the hole's perimeter. The foundation must have been two floors deep into the ground.

Bodjie filled everyone in. "They were building the covered court here. It was a sunken basketball court and auditorium."

To the rest of us, it was a crater in the muddy brown soil. The drainage ports looked like a dizzying labyrinth puzzle waiting to be solved.

Bodjie had the inside scoop once again. "The developers were aware of flooding risks. They planned to install the large cylindrical ports to improve drainage during flashfloods. It didn't fall through because the budget ran dry, ain't that right?"

"Didn't even get started," I answered.

"This place looks scary," Laleng suddenly said. She hugged herself, not due to the cold. It was warm and muggy, but the place gave her the creeps.

"Isn't it beautiful?" Bodjie said, smiling, proud of his find.

Enrico sneered. "What's so scary about all this?"

"Come on! Is it hide-and-seek you want?" Bodjie cried.

"Watch it! There's so much mud you could slip and get mud all over your clothes," I told them.

"What game do we play?" Jason asked.

Everyone waited for me to speak. "Hide-and-seek," I said. "Whoever's tagged must find at least one of us. The objective is to outlast the others or make it back to home base so you can be safe."

"Me," Bodjie declared. "I'm it!"

Bodjie got in position by turning his back to us and standing against a tree. He covered his eyes with his arms and counted to twenty, while we all sprinted away from the corner of the lot. I scanned the property, looking for a hiding place that would be safe.

Found one.

I made my way past many drainage ports, many blocks of stacked up concrete, skirting around networks of steel beams climbing the ground like pillars without busts. My shoes slushed in the mud. My books and pens clattered in my backpack the faster I went.

My hiding place wasn't a large cylindrical block, but a slice of pavement with a manhole cover. I lifted the heavy steel lid and struggled to push it open. Then, I heaved with everything I had, and it budged. I hopped in and slid it shut from behind.

I couldn't hear anything from above. It was dark down there, muddy, wet, cooler because it was closed off from the sun. There were a few rats, and there was water flowing down the tunnel. I shone a flashlight and peered into the darkness. A tunnel led into a larger drain—bars filtered large objects from passing through, like trash in the sewage.

The muddy subterranean tunnel was brown and black, like sludge and humus coated the walls. The water stunk of sewage; I was used to it though. After all, I was a scavenger.

I pointed the flashlight forward, reaching the iron bars where the water flowed out. It extended to an even larger sewer below where dirty water flowed at the speed of a small river. Chunks of feces, decaying food particles, and bits of refuse traveled down the roaring pitch-black stream toward the unseen.

The rats were partly mad at my interloping into their world. They hissed at me, and I backed off so I wouldn't be bitten, then returned to my spot below the cistern. No one called out and said the game was over, so panic set in. I decided to find my way back to home base, but when I attempted to slide the cistern open, it wouldn't budge.

It was stuck, so I panicked, cried out. "Help! Bodjie! Laleng! Jason! Enrico! Come and help me!"

My nightmare down below grew even worse when the flashlight began flickering. It eventually ran out of batteries, and all around me grew dark. It felt like a tomb, and there I was, clawing and pushing at the steel manhole cover, screaming, frantically heaving at the slab of steel with all my might.

It was maybe twenty to thirty minutes down in that darkness before someone figured out that I had gone down the manhole. During that seemingly infinite amount of time, my heart raced, and I sweated profusely. Things moved in the shadows at the end of the tunnel, rose from the drainage port and seeped through, reconstituting into ghostly apparitions made of fecal matter and decay. I imagined a haggardly person peering at me through the drainage port, their yellow-green eyes watching me hungrily.

Jason called out from above. "Min! Are you down there?"

I screamed, bashed on the heavy steel platelet with my fists to make noises.

"Hey! He's down here!" Jason called out.

Together with Bodjie and Enrico, Jason pushed the manhole cover open. It had apparently wedged stuck when I closed it against the lid in a perfect fit.

With a big breath, I welcomed the fresh air and daylight. I climbed out with Bodjie's help, and they all looked at me, relieved.

"We looked everywhere!"

Jason spoke up. "We thought you went home. It's a good thing we didn't stop searching."

Laleng shook her head at me. "You almost got buried alive."

It didn't take long for all of them to laugh.

"What do you say? Speech!"

It was my turn to laugh. "Thanks, guys! Thank you, really. Man, was I scared shitless!"

"You stink, as usual," Bodjie said.

Enrico slapped me on the shoulder. "Come on! Let's go! Min might think twice about returning to that sewer!"

We went home, but I never forgot that place. Weeks later, its relevance would come back to me. The horror that would take Tondo by storm was just brewing.

CHAPTER 3

DRUGS

As fires raged in Tondo, Manila, and I scarcely had a place to go, I hid in small, dark rooms in empty houses, with bolt locks on the doors for safety. Always, hunger would keep me moving, keep me searching for a better place. When I ran into zombies, my quick feet would skitter on the broken sidestreets, like Pegasus had gifted my ankles with wings.

Never did the promise of food justify the sacrifice of leaving a safe hideout. Never did the satisfaction of a full stomach placate the fear. Always, zombies would come flying out of nowhere, screeching like banshees wailing, just as hungry as I was.

It was exhausting, dodging zombies in the food market on the Radial Road R-10 where they lay in ambush. It was frustrating, sleeping with one eye open, and learning to do it, literally for survival's sake. I never thought I could. I was so fatigued, yet scared of being a zombie's dinner, it became second nature.

The promise of a quick meal via a fruit hanging from a tree by the roadside proved tempting. Still, I looked around, trying to calculate the time needed to climb the tree and get down. Imagine if I made the climb and was surrounded by zombies while up there. I couldn't fathom that any death would be more painful, or terrifying. This was the world's end scripted in the twenty-first century. All deaths were bound to be excruciating, whether by contracting disease and getting eaten or fighting to survive and experiencing the same.

How did the zombie outbreak start? Picture a group of primitive druggies crouched over paraphernalia on the floor of a dark room in a shanty. See the smoke leave the empty plastic straw they used to inhale the vapor from a charred substance coating a silver spoon. Now, imagine the druggies take in a deep breath, snorting all signs of white smoke, throwing their heads back, eyes half-closed showing nothing but the whites; the smiles on their faces registering contentment, bliss; their muscles stretching taut over their bones; their blood vessels growing larger, darker; their fingers bonier, their fingernails sharper and colored with death.

Inside the darkest rooms all over Tondo, these drug buddies congregated secretly, each hit of *shabu* bringing them closer to becoming undead. How? No one knew. Everyone, including the government, was puzzled. I asked my friend, Doctor Amorsolo, about it numerous times and he was similarly perplexed.

Looking back...

Doctor Amorsolo would volunteer time at the free clinic just a short walk from our shanties at Barangay Happyland. When pressed for answers, he would speak freely about the drug problem, why the situation went beyond control, why people turned to something so ruinous as to forfeit their lives.

It was a weekend at the free clinic—a mobile trailer where a doctor and nurse set up equipment to treat indigent patients. Once a week they camped outside Barangay Happyland along the Radial Road R-10 for residents. I had an interesting conversation with the doc before the zombie outbreak started. He explained the reasons behind the up-ward-trending drug use and the best ways to combat it.

"The problem isn't the drugs, Min. It's mental illness that's wreaking havoc on populations that are burdened by great economic hardship, and it's prompting people to find a desperate means to cope," he said. Doctor Amorsolo was fifty-three, a husband and father of four. His thinning, graying, straight hair was combed to one side, and his com-plexion was a smooth, dusty white, showing a hint of Chinese ancestry. He often prescribed antibiotics and other medications to my mama and papa. Doctor Amorsolo also took care of my health check-ups, and smiled like a family doctor happy to volunteer for the plight of poor people.

"I think the solution to drugs is education, Luzvimindo," he con-tinued. "With an education, you have opportunities to get ahead, work abroad, work in a corporate office, or even start your own business. It's harder to climb out of poverty if you're forced to work blue-collar jobs with no sustainable development.

"If the masses were educated, the eighty percent of the population living in poverty would be drastically reduced. Suddenly, these folks can get professional opportunities, not jobs scavenging or begging for alms or simply relying on charities. It starts with the children. The chil-dren need to be assured of a clear path to education: advanced reading, writing, and math skills to help them compete with employees in the global marketplace. Sadly, Filipinos like you are overlooked by our cor-rupt government. Politicians only care about shady deals, overpricing, pocketing taxpayer money, and not giving back to poorer communities. They satisfy their wealthy constituents. Come election time, they sing praises to the masses. But afterward, it's all a joke.

"Remember that, Min. Stay in school and graduate. Forgetting your problems or numbing your pain isn't going to solve anything," he said with emphasis, like an uncle would.

"Doc," I said, looking up as he noted my blood pressure reading on my chart before loosening the cuff. "Why are so many kids giving up? Why quit school so young? My friends and I all want to graduate."

Doctor Amorsolo looked solemn, and patted me on the shoulder. "They didn't finish because they had to care for their families. Or because some kids don't have your perseverance. I hope that someday you won't have to work scavenging landfills anymore, Luzvimindo. See how sick it makes you?"

He took a saliva sample with a cotton bud then placed it in a bag, which he stored in a locked compartment.

"Yes, Doctor," I said. He gave me a lollipop, and I got out of the chair. He patted me on the shoulder again and told me everything was fine.

"Until we meet again, Min. Take care of yourself. Say hi to your parents for me."

"Yes, Doctor. I want to be a doctor, too, someday. Goodbye for now."

"Luzvimindo, stay away from pushers. Say no," he said one last time before I turned to leave.

Little did I know that the *shabu* epidemic would reach a breaking point, and the drugs would start turning addicts into blood-crazed zombies. Doctor Amorsolo's thoughts on the drug epidemic described a society in decline. Who knew that all-out catastrophe was waiting?

The line at the clinic was long, but I was glad to have had my conversation with Doctor Amorsolo. Work beckoned, as usual, and I went to meet friends to go scavenging at our landfill in Happyland.

Jason didn't need to scavenge like the rest of us. He lived somewhere better—a concrete, three-story house with a rooftop patio near his old school at Barangay 116. His dad owned a motorcycle repair shop, and his mom employed seamstresses to do alterations. Clothes hung from the rooftop patio in view of the street below. They didn't have a yard. Jason had three siblings, and they shared rooms. Their parents slept in the master bedroom. The house was still like the Ritz compared to the shanties.

Bodjie, Enrico, Laleng, and I walked down the Radial Road R-10 to the landfill. Food carts scattered across both sides of the streets, where benches full of customers crowded the food stalls. Just a short walk away, despite the heavy thoroughfare on R-10, the sidestreets leading to the landfill looked abandoned. Construction workers were building more shanties nearby. We passed them by in our t-shirts and pairs of shorts, skipping over mud puddles in our ragged flip flops.

We joked, nudged each other, and laughed. When we finally diverged from the main road and trudged down a dirt road muddied by large dump truck tires and incessant rain, we picked up the scent of the landfill on the breeze.

"Still rather far, you can already smell the site," Enrico said.

"Just what Min's future wife is going to smell like," Bodjie quipped.

"More like your wife, Bodjie," I said, lightly jabbing at his ribs with my elbow.

We laughed harder. As we neared, more and more scavengers came from the direction of the site. They were pushing *kariton,* primitive wooden carts that were filled with bags stuffed full of scavenged material. They were dressed in little more than stained, soiled rags. They wrapped torn, discarded, oversized clothing or old towels or blankets around their waists and used them as loincloths. Their skin was olive dark, smeared brown and bruised blue and black with the toil of daily rote. Their jaundiced eyes spoke of defeat. Yet, they smiled at their loved ones, offered the tender touch of a hand mussing a young one's hair—a hand just used to forage the city's mountains of garbage.

The kids retained an innocence that was lost on adults. They beamed while at play, just like I did with Bodjie and the others a while back. Looking into the eyes of those who suffered most in Happyland's landfills was a test of wills. Only cold hearts would not be moved to give something, anything. Yet, the kids and adults here never begged. This was the life and circumstances they were used to. I didn't know a different kind of life. Some scavengers still sought help at free clinics for symptoms similar to leprosy. That, and the world of fatal diseases to which they were constantly exposed.

When we arrived, there was a small crowd dispersed across the landfill, scavenging before the rains could make the work that much harder.

We waded through damp refuse. It soaked our feet, ankles, and shins. Sometimes, we were submerged knee-deep in loose garbage. We used the rods to maintain balance, to help us get free and get back up. We picked up aluminum cans, foil. We gathered old ketchup bottles, jelly jars. We dropped them into our bags, then we slung the bags over our shoulders. We prodded relentlessly with our sticks to identify resalable trash, not wasting time because we would have to take our haul to the junkshop to turn in for cash. Then, we would make our way home.

I was scouring for what I could when suddenly the ground came out from underneath me. I yelped. Slipped past a hard trap door and slid down a flight of steps into a room in the ground. I groaned as I checked my ankle and glanced at my surroundings for a brief second. Muddy walls were held in place by *yero*. The latter had obscene words scrawled in graffiti. Thankfully, the pain subsided quickly. The shelter must have belonged to a scavenger. When I glanced around one more time to see whether said scavenger was here, I found a man shaking uncontrollably on the ground close by, wearing little more than a soiled pair of shorts.

He was sweating. His eyes were oscillating, moving rapidly like he was possessed, like he was in violent REM sleep, or like he was in shock.

But then I saw the teaspoon, lighter, and plastic straw nearby, and it all added up. He was overdosing. Frothing at the mouth, saliva and foam leaking out of the corners. He'd also let go of his bowels. A small puddle of urine trailed from his crotch area, and a mound of soft, wet feces leaked from the back of his shorts and coated his thighs.

I clambered out of the hole, screaming for my friends. When I reached the opening, I took a big gulp of air and filled my lungs with toxic vapor. My gut churned with nausea.

Bodjie came. Then Laleng. Then Enrico. Most of the scavengers didn't pay any heed. Just went about their business. I pointed to the open trap door in the ground, and Bodjie investigated.

He came up shortly after, eyes wide with panic.

"Is he still convulsing?" I asked. "What do we do?"

"He's slowing down, and his eyes are no longer moving. He's as good as dead. He won't make it to the hospital."

Laleng patted me on the shoulder. Enrico asked me if I was fine. We called out to some scavengers who walked close by and told them that a man was lying down there, overdosing.

One of them went down, soon returning and yelling for the others to call for help.

"We'll take it from here. You kids go on home before it rains," one of them told us.

We gathered our bags and left for the junkshop. On our way out, a scream tore loose from behind. We kept going even though terror gripped us. We knew something terrible had happened. The man who was overdosing wasn't dead yet.

When we arrived at the junkshop, we unslung our bags and placed them on top of the tables for weighing. The junkshop staff sorted the items inside and placed them on scales, and they paid us accordingly. Along the way home, walking on the street by the bay, I locked eyes with notorious Tondo drug pusher and addict, Danilo Vargas, smoking outside a store. He nodded at me and smiled. He looked like a bag of bones, dark brown skin hiding thin strips of muscle, eyes cutting through innocent smiles. We were quiet the rest of the way.

When I got home, Mama and Papa were very concerned about the day's proceedings. They made me promise not to take drugs.

"I promise," I told them. I was certain.

———— ◦ ————

Our neighbors were friends of my father. They were gone just as often, traveling to construction sites to work. Mang Rudy, single, forty-seven years old, lived across from us. Mang Ric, widowed, fifty-nine, lived next door. They were nice people; they looked out for me whenever they were home. "Are you doing well in school, Min?" Mang Rudy would inquire. "No bullies?"

"None," I'd say.

Mang Ric's family lived in the province. Mang Rudy never married; he liked to eat, drink, and laugh a lot with friends. Both were simple people like us. They didn't demand more than what life gave them.

It was Mang Ric who knocked on our door the day after we had found the overdosing scavenger. Papa was still home, resting from his job at the construction site, and so was Mang Rudy. The two men were outside in the hallway when Papa answered the door.

Mang Ric looked troubled. Mang Rudy stood in the open doorway of his room across from ours.

Papa read their faces. "What seems to be the problem?" he asked. "What's wrong?"

Mang Ric turned to face Mang Rudy, who encouraged his friend to speak, but Mang Ric didn't lift the burdened look on his face. He glanced at my mama and myself then summoned the courage. "My son, Dionisio, from our province of Laguna was caught doing drugs," he said. Mang Ric looked down, eyes welling up. He looked back up at Papa. "He ran from the law."

Papa comforted Mang Ric. "Don't worry so much. Do you know where he is?"

"No," Mang Ric said with a shake of his head.

Mang Rudy joined in. "He might come here."

Papa looked at Mama, and the two tried their best not to overreact as they comforted Mang Ric. "If he comes here, do you want us to tell him to surrender to the authorities so he doesn't aggravate his case further?"

Mang Ric didn't look comforted. The next thing he said was even harder to say—he struggled through the words. "Hope is lost. He's killed someone." Mang Ric paused to stifle tears, but he wasn't done yet. "Dionisio looked different; his cheeks were gaunt, eyes yellow, gums dark. Words couldn't dissuade him, like his mind had gone."

We stood silent as Mang Ric wept. Mang Rudy held him by the shoulder, and Papa patted him on the back. Mama reached out and hugged him. I did too. We weren't saying it, but we were just as scared that Dionisio would come looking for trouble in Happyland, maybe to see his father and steal money for stash.

Or worse.

CHAPTER 4

BODJIE TAKES DRUGS

The days leading to my escape out of Tondo, I did the best I could to stay alive. Ducking before I could be seen, running before I could get caught, I was one step ahead of the zombies, one breath from annihilation.

Alone and desperate, I pulled every trick in the book I knew. I was street-smart, wise. I ran out of houses with my arms full of loot, my legs propelled by fear, fatigue a faraway thing.

I would stop somewhere, tear the wrapper off my candy bar, chomp the top end. Eyes wide, sweat dripping from my forehead, I was on the lookout for zombies, careful not to get cornered.

During stops in between runs searching for food, I recalled Bodjie and the others, sadness filling me. Bodjie was my closest friend, the guy I counted on to have my back. I knew Laleng would leave the country someday. I knew Bodjie would always stay. He loved our country, loved the good times we shared, joking and laughing.

As I kept my distance from zombie-infested places, I couldn't help but feel alone, like I was the last person left in the world. Bodjie had always given me his loyalty, his friendship. Once, during the zombie outbreak, I passed the Vitas Bridge, where his home used to be. I found the debris left behind by the violence, the wooden clapboards and personal effects washed aside by the water. I peered at the empty space under the bridge where his home had been attached and felt emptiness. Emptiness and despair.

Remembering him was a diversion. Remembering all my friends brought equal parts comfort and pain. There seemed to be no place safe from the zombies, not even to sleep a full eight hours and dream fondly, escape. Always, there would be a racket somewhere, the clawing of dead fingernails against the locked steel gate, the hoarse cry of a zombie moved by intense hunger, somehow sniffing for fresh blood, sensing my presence in a room with an open window, where I awaited, shuddering. Although I always wound up wrong, as the zombies would leave, I would never forget the fear gripping my bones, the cold, damp sweat despite the heat. I would move on to look for food. Always looking ahead, behind, all around...

I kept moving, recalling the friends I had lost.

⸻

I used to meet with my friends at school—Jason, Bodjie, Enrico, and Laleng. Being on the run in an attempt to survive made me miss them. I, therefore, recalled school, when life was fun, easier. We didn't want to fall behind and graduate late. Education was our ticket. The sooner we could get good jobs and raise our families from squalor, the better. Jason wanted to be a racecar driver. Bodjie wanted to be an executive. Enrico wanted to be an engineer. Laleng wanted to be a nurse and work abroad.

I wanted to be a doctor. "Is that what you want to be when you grow up?" Mama had asked me, seemingly in disbelief.

I nodded and smiled. She smiled back tenderly, like she was proud. Papa also smiled proudly; it was as if I had just soothed their many aches and pains in life.

"I won't forget you when the time comes, Mama and Papa."

Papa put an arm around Mama and then mussed my hair. Mama hugged me.

"We will rise," I said to them.

I was, therefore, serious with my studies. As a sixth grader, there were bad apples—students that rebelled by experimenting with cigarettes, drinking, drugs.

I didn't. I remembered Mama and Papa. Even though it hurt to see that other classmates could afford gadgets like smartphones bought from the black market—no doubt stolen—I told myself that one day, I would have a chance to afford cool stuff.

We were back in school one day, standing outside one of the second-floor classrooms with my friends, when Bodjie gestured toward some kids headed to the back of the grade school building, just behind the carpentry room. "Maybe they're using *shabu* over there," he said. He sounded regretful, like he was missing out.

I chastised him. "Don't you dare think about it, Bodjie! It will be like coming to a stop right on the train tracks."

"I was just saying," he snapped back, still grimacing like he was envious.

Laleng glared. Enrico sneered. Jason looked hesitant.

"Hey!" Laleng said. "Don't be stupid! You'll ruin all your future plans by doing drugs!"

Bodjie scratched his head and nodded. He was being the crazy guy, the guy who wanted to try things because he pretended not to know better.

But I *did* know better, and I felt sorry for those other kids.

Classes went by as usual. Nothing notable. Except that Bodjie got approached by a couple of the varsity batchmates we saw behind the carpentry room. I asked Bodjie if he was fine, and he said he was. Word around campus was that the two batchmates were fraternity neophytes looking to recruit others. I thought of bugging Bodjie about it, but he was being evasive. He just shook his head and looked the other way.

The same guys who had approached Bodjie also chatted Jason up later that day. He nodded and exchanged smiles and laughs with them. They fist bumped, and I sensed trouble brewing.

So, who did I tell?

Laleng, of course.

"Hey, Doña. I have something to tell you."

She smiled. Her two other friends giggled, like Laleng and I were an item suddenly. "What is it, Min?" she asked as I led her out of earshot.

"Jason and Bodjie were approached by frat guys. The ones who were huddled at the back of the carpentry room a while back. I have a bad feeling about it."

"What did they say?" Laleng asked, brow creasing with concern.

"Bodjie sort of denied it. I haven't warned Jason yet. Maybe Jason and Bodjie are just doing their best to get along."

"Let's talk about it after class. The bell just rang, Min! Come on, we have to go! Where are they?"

I looked around but couldn't find them. "Maybe they went ahead. Everybody has gotten out of their seat."

"Okay," Laleng said. "Let's meet up with them later. Don't worry, Min."

I hurried to get my things, brushing past others who were leaving for the next class. With every glance around campus, I found no sign of Bodjie and Jason...or the boys who had approached them. Worry churned my gut as I looked around, but when I arrived at the next class, Jason was there, waiting. I sighed in relief and took my seat next to him. Bodjie scrambled in right after the teacher entered and made it to his seat without getting questioned. His forehead was sweaty, and he smiled at Jason and I before facing the blackboard. I had a sinking feeling Bodjie was making some very bad decisions.

———

After final dismissal, we met up at the benches beside the gate as usual. Everyone was there except Bodjie. Where was he? My paranoia was getting the better of me, so I told the others.

"He was late earlier. Didn't I tell you guys something was up? Jason, what did those guys tell you when they approached you?"

"Introduced themselves. Because I'm new, they said. They asked who my favorite basketball player was, so I told them I was a fan of Michael Jordan. I played it safe!"

"That's all?"

"Yes. Like you don't believe me or something."

It was Laleng's turn to worry. "Maybe Bodjie is just late."

"He's the instigator. He's always here by this time to hang out," Enrico said.

"You guys go on. Go home. I'll look for him," I told them. They were hesitant, wanting to look for him too.

"Min, we'll come too," Laleng answered.

"Never mind him," Enrico complained. "Let's just leave."

"Please go ahead," I said again.

Jason, Laleng, and Enrico quietly agreed.

"I'll look. Just around here on campus. He couldn't have left before we arrived. We've been waiting by the gate all this time."

———

I stood alone, facing the long driveway that cut through the grounds. The campus was quiet. The sounds of other kids screaming, laughing, and cheering erupted occasionally, breaking the silence. Like me, they hung out before heading home for the day. Laleng and Enrico had left for the landfill to scavenge. Jason had gone home. So I set out to look for Bodjie. Where could he be? I kept my eyes peeled for the boys who'd approached him as I made my way up the driveway, peering into each downstairs classroom. Bodjie was still on campus, but where?

One dark, quiet classroom after another, I peeked inside. When rooms were too dark, I turned the lights on very briefly, shining bright fluorescent light on empty chairs, empty blackboards, and empty teacher's tables. The chairs were in disarray. The school janitor would go through each room and arrange them for classes the next day. Right now, disquiet brooded like an ominously dark pool of water. The school looked haunted at the end of the day, ghosts of previous generations still leaving their mark.

I remembered chalk scrawled on blackboards, words half-erased, equations unsolved. I peered out the windows of the classrooms on the first floor to see if Bodjie and the other kids could have been hiding behind the building. If they were crouched low behind the wall, I wouldn't see them; I would have to circle around the back.

There was no one in the first-floor classrooms, and I peered into the library just in time to hear the announcement that it was closing, so I headed to the carpentry room next—the farthest room on the entire campus. The small veranda at the rear of the room held flowering santan and hibiscus bushes, as good a place as any for schoolmates to hide. The three boys I'd seen earlier today often headed here.

No one.

Nothing.

No drug paraphernalia. No cigarette butts.

The carpentry room had been tidied for the next day. Still no Bodjie, but there was a restroom next to Mr. Sevilla's office. He would have gone for the day, and none of the other students would have used it past dismissal time.

The entrance was narrow. It was dark beyond. The bathroom was only used by Mr. Sevilla and students during carpentry classes.

I stepped into the darkness of the bathroom, and there was Bodjie, shivering on the floor. Shivering and sweating profusely in his uniform. He had also urinated in his pants and vomited on his shirt. The room stunk.

Next to his clenched hand was an empty plastic wrapper, a burnt match, and a sliver of scorched aluminum foil caked with a black, crusty substance.

CHAPTER 5

THE TRANSFORMATION

Bodjie was expelled from school, and it did not take long for Laleng, Enrico, Jason, and all our classmates to hear the news he had been taken to the hospital. He was recovering, and doctors said he was going to be fine. Visitors weren't allowed, but the family told us that I could see him. After all, I had found him on the floor of the bathroom, overdosing, which meant I had saved his life. I was supposed to be a hero. Yet, I was anxious to see how he was doing.

When I stepped out of the elevator onto the charity ward in Tondo General Hospital, the hallways were crowded with patients. Stretchers lined the outside of the Emergency Room and the hallways of the ICUs. The charity wing was overflowing. The staff did their best to stabilize COVID cases and quarantine them at home instead. Yet, every day an influx of new infections flooded the understaffed infirmary. Bodjie's family told us that he would spend the rest of his recovery time at their house once he was ready.

Bodjie was awake when I entered the room. His parents smiled and left. I saw that Bodjie was upset, and I tried my best to cheer him up.

"Well? How are you? You'll get out soon enough. Just two or three days now."

"Then what? Go back to school? That's gone! I must go to work now."

"Why did you take drugs? You knew what would happen to you."

Bodjie stared out the window. He was my best friend, and he threw his future away as early as sixth grade. Gone were his dreams of working in corporate offices, wearing his smart suit and tie, or driving his car or SUV.

I felt sorry for him, but I was also angry. I had warned him not to do drugs. And what did he do? Bought a stash of *shabu* from the other boys and then overdosed. Worst of all, he didn't rat out the drug pushers. These were actual pushers in sixth grade, doing drugs! The school promised to absolve him and suspend him if he would tell on the runners, but Bodjie didn't want to be a snitch. Truly a dumbass, indeed!

"What's wrong, Bodjie? What was the problem? It was like you ruined everything for no reason. Why did you take drugs?"

Bodjie continued to stare out the window, refusing to face me. "Dad might lose his job, and he doesn't have any money to buy a motorcycle so he can be a tricycle driver or food delivery rider. My mom sells goods at a small store. She can't feed all four of us in the family. Dad has been coming home drunk of late. Sometimes, he yells at us. I fear for my family. I need to be brave."

I felt so bad for Bodjie, but it still wasn't answer enough. I needed to know why he would turn to drugs to drown his troubles. Drugs only made matters worse.

"I didn't plan on getting hooked or overdosing on my stash. I planned on working as a runner," he said.

"Forget what happened, Bodjie. Just report the pushers to the principal so you can attend school again. Please, Bodjie. While you still can." I continued, "Have pity on yourself and your family!"

"They might kill me *or* my family!" Bodjie cried, eyes bulging wide as he spat venom at me.

What he said next made me regret that he was ever my friend. I was shocked. Yes, maybe he had problems at home. Maybe he was sick of scavenging at the landfill. Maybe he wanted to be a runner or pusher, make some extra cash to buy a smartphone or some new clothes. Surely, telling on a few sixth-grade pushers wouldn't endanger his family. But they had warned him sternly, and he had believed them. They were frat neophytes, so they would have claimed to have ties with many members and their networks. They would have threatened him precisely like he said they did. Bodjie gave his word that he wouldn't tell. Then, he stupidly took too much of the drugs with them in the bathroom and overdosed. The other kids got spooked and took off. He spent all his recent scavenging earnings on the small stash. He should have said no. Simple.

"It's your fault, Luzvimindo! I never should have befriended you. You're too much of a baby about things like this."

He glared out the window, like all of this had somehow been my doing.

<hr />

Laleng, Enrico, Jason, and I were in school the day after I visited Bodjie, and they were just as shocked as I was.

"Is that what he said? Wasn't he grateful that you saved his life? What an asshole!"

Jason rubbed his forehead with a sigh.

Enrico shuffled his feet and spoke next. "He fucking does drugs, man, and he's angry at you? Bodjie is such a weirdo! What a weirdo!"

I grieved at the loss of my friend. I was still a bit angry, but his future was in jeopardy. We had to help him. Even if he was expelled from school. "Let's just help him. Let's pitch in. We can help Bodjie find another school."

Jason seconded me. "Right, guys. Let's just help him. For now, let's help him recover in good spirits. If he'll need a job, let's ask around."

Suddenly, a group of guys walked by, and we all fell into silence. They were the boys who approached Bodjie the day he went missing, the day I had found him overdosing in the restroom after school.

The biggest kid's name was Jet, our star varsity basketball player. They called him "Jet" because he had explosive moves. He demonstrated it by walking past in a blur and bumping me hard on the shoulder, nearly knocking me to the ground.

"Motherfucker! Do you have a problem?" he sneered, clenching his hands like he was ready for a fight. "What? You want to fight me?"

The other two boys looked on, smiling. The second boy was big around the waist. We knew him as Boyba, derived from "baboy," the Tagalog word for pig.

"Guy's a coward. You can take him," Boyba said, flipping me off.

The last boy was tall like Jet but all skin and bones; he was also a varsity player. He liked to pop his knuckles a lot, like he was always ready for a brawl. He went by his real name, Emerson, instead of a street name because he liked to think of himself as a fil-foreign player.

"What, you little twerps? Haven't you been in a fight before?" Emerson taunted.

Enrico started to sweat. Jason stepped back. I was frozen in my shoes, thinking I was about to be beaten to a pulp. It was Laleng who stepped to the frontline.

"We'll report you for starting trouble! Do you want to get suspended or expelled? Just go ahead!"

Jet, Emerson, and Boyba just laughed at us.

"*Putang ina*!" Jet said. "Motherfuckers! You're a bunch of snitches! Stay the hell away! We don't want you to start crying to Mama."

They swaggered away, so sure of themselves. Enrico, Laleng, and Jason comforted me. However, I took special notice of Laleng. Enrico and Jason swooned.

"Yiheeeee!" they both said as I smiled at Laleng for getting in between me and the bullies. It was too bad those guys had gotten to Bodjie, but while I was still angry with him, I was glad he was recovering. Now, though, we realized that we had to watch our backs.

It was Laleng who pointed out something about those goons, and she was right. They were making jittery movements with their arms, like they were anxious, and the skin on their hands was thin and heavily veined. Lines and black patches were showing under their eyelids. Their lips were dark and chapped. Their fingernails and teeth were stained a deep yellow.

They were addicts.

They were just twelve years old.

———————————

After dismissal time, we headed home. Jason went ahead; he lived south of our school's location, and had to split off like usual. The rest of us walked a different route.

Laleng lived in a shanty community closest to campus. When we arrived at her street, she walked into a narrow passageway accessible from a store, a *tindahan* that sold snacks and food ingredients on the street corner. Her house was on the second floor of a shanty; from the outside, it looked just like mine. She slept in a small room with her three siblings while her parents slept in an adjacent room that only had space for a bed. Her mom waved at us from the second-floor window—we'd known her since we were little.

After seeing Laleng home, Enrico and I finally crossed the Radial Road R-10 via the overpass and went farther up the bay, north of Barangay Happyland. His home was on a shanty overlooking the water. Behind a small green gate and a small yard, a tiny concrete house fit for only one person stood crammed next to others. Enrico, his two siblings, and his parents all slept in one room. When Enrico reached the green gate, he rushed into the waiting arms of his youngest sibling, still a toddler. He was delighted. With a wave and a smile, I headed home, dragging my feet with fatigue.

On my own, I braved the long walk down the Radial Road R-10 into Barangay Happyland's muddy, pothole-and-garbage-ridden two-lane streets, making my way to my shanty by the bay.

The hair on my neck rose suddenly, and my stomach dropped. With a sense of dread, I turned around.

I didn't know what hit me.

<hr />

My breath was punched out of me, pain shooting through my sternum. I fell to the ground, clutching my mid-section and willing away my nausea. When I looked up, Jet was standing over me, grinning. The other two boys arrived and rained down punches on my head. Then they kicked me about my body while I tried to protect myself. Finally, Jet grabbed me by the hair and yanked me to my feet. Boyba grabbed me from behind, and Emerson punched me in the gut again.

This time, I vomited.

"Now what, motherfucker? Don't you be ratting us out. You're nothing but a snitch!"

My ears were ringing. My head was spinning. But I knew Jet's voice. Still, before Jet or Emerson could inflict further punishment, a loud scream erupted behind me, and I suddenly fell to the ground, free.

Boyba was grabbing his shoulder and neck area, blood seeping through his fingers. On the ground at his feet, drug addict and pusher Danilo Vargas spasmed, frothing blood and foam at the mouth, eyes yellow, teeth bright red, veins dark blue like oil ran through them.

It couldn't be.

What had happened to him? My initial thought was that he had saved me, but I was scared shitless all the same. Jet and Emerson backed off and begged for Vargas' mercy. "But, sir! We're just following your orders. We'll go now!"

Jet and Emerson made a dash for it, but Vargas made a last-ditch effort to reach for Boyba's leg. He held on mightily, even as Boyba fought to get free. Boyba begged for his life; he cried like a child. That was when Vargas bit into Boyba's shin, drawing blood, stripping meat from bone.

Boyba screamed.

I ran.

Before I could get far, the police arrived and surrounded them. They aimed their guns at Vargas and called for him to release Boyba.

Vargas didn't.

The police didn't warn him again.

Bullets pierced the air as cops from all sides fired at Vargas in the middle of the narrow intersection. Gunshots tore through flesh. Vargas shook on the ground as blood spattered. When he stopped shaking, everyone fell silent, almost like they were waiting for Vargas to come back to life again.

One cop, then another, moved in slowly. Fingers were placed to a neck before a signal was given.

He was dead. And I knew it.

A crowd had gathered, watching in awe. Boyba was howling in pain. Vargas had taken a big chunk out of Boyba's shoulder and another from his leg, exposing bone and causing him to bleed profusely. The police appeared hesitant to help him, almost as though they knew he was a drug pusher and thus refused. The cops looked at Vargas with disgust.

"Motherfucking addicts!" one officer said. The other cops shook their heads.

I was still mystified. Vargas didn't just look like an addict. He looked like a zombie.

Weeks went by. Jason, Enrico, Laleng, and I felt safer in school now that Jet and the others had been expelled for beating me up. Boyba was treated for his injuries, but was suffering significant trauma after the Vargas incident. The three boys would spend time in the detention center for starting the fracas; since they were minors, they couldn't be imprisoned.

We also learned that Jet, Boyba, and Emerson had problems at home. Just like Bodjie did.

But our focus was on Bodjie and his job situation. We tried to help him get one. Jason inquired with his dad, but Bodjie didn't know a thing about motorcycles. Laleng asked her dad whether Bodjie could assist him servicing air conditioner units. Enrico's dad was a tricycle driver, so he couldn't do much for Bodjie either. I asked my mom whether Bodjie could work at the canteen, buying food and supplies from the market or something—she asked, but the owner refused.

No luck. Nobody wanted to give Bodjie a chance. Everyone knew that he had done drugs, and no one wanted to associate with him. He was off-limits.

So, Bodjie scavenged at the landfill full-time, hoping to find rare metals like gold and copper in the trash. He was downcast, but he tried to get on with his life. At least, that's what we thought.

A few weeks after Bodjie started scavenging all day at the dumpsite, traveling from the landfill with a *kariton*, filling the wooden cart with his finds to take to the junkshop and then back again, we seldom saw him. We decided to check on him one day when we were doing our own scavenging at the site, but it appeared Bodjie was purposely avoiding us.

We waited for him at the entrance, staking him and his *kariton* out. Then, he finally showed. He had shriveled. His *sando* and shorts exposed his bony arms, thighs, the sharp angles of his shoulders, and sunken torso. His calves were stilts. His fingers looked like toothpicks. His eyes were deep yellow, red lines zigzagging across the corneas. Prominent veins patterned his brown skin.

He breathed hard while pushing his cart. His mouth was open; the tender, lean meat on his arms and shoulders contracted and released with great strain; his legs pushed against the ground with the heavy plopping sound of his sandals. He stared straight ahead, ignoring us. We called out to him, and he said nothing. He just focused ahead like we weren't there.

"Bodjie, *kumusta na*? You look like you've lost a bunch of weight!" I said to him, speaking up so he could hear me. I was certain he would answer, but he didn't muster a response. It sure looked like he was mad. There was something different about him as well. Like he was barely there, barely conscious of any of us. Like the light in his eyes had died, his cheeks, jaw, eyes, nose, and teeth looking diseased, his whole body defeated. I felt sorry for him, for what this hard life was doing to my friend.

When he continued to ignore us, Laleng took exception. "Wow!" she said. "He's a snob now. He did drugs, dug himself a hole, and now we're to blame."

Enrico laughed. I was unsure whether he was resentful or whether he was just laughing at Bodjie out of cynicism. Jason just smiled sarcastically. I told them to stop it.

"Guys, he looks like he's changed a lot. Let's follow him from a distance and just check on him."

We did. For some time. He scrounged for trash and placed it in his *kariton* and we followed like stalkers, dodging from rubbish pile to rubbish pile. Finally, we watched him climb a large mound of garbage on the edge of the landfill and find a spot to sit.

Moments later, he took out some stuff from his cart: a white powdery substance in a tiny plastic bag, a jagged section of tin pieced off from a soda can, and a gas lighter.

We watched in horror as he placed the powder on the sectioned canister, then lit up. He breathed in the fumes, closed his eyes in contentment, and smiled like a dazed, deranged man—even though he was just twelve years old like the rest of us.

Once he was finished, he got back to his feet and started moving quicker, jumping from one solid footing of trash to another like a lithe athlete.

Back at school the next day, we were sad that Bodjie had lost his way but serious about our studies because we didn't want to end up like him.

Jason, Enrico, and I went to carpentry class with our kits, and marveled over the portfolio we had in the display room.

We met up with Laleng after she was done with crafts class. She was artistic. "Too bad," I said after seeing her project. "It's too bad you want to be a nurse, Laleng."

"I want to work abroad. No buts," she said.

Enrico laughed. "No *butts,* you said? How about..." he said, pointing at her behind.

She giggled, then slapped Enrico along the arm when he wouldn't stop laughing. Jason and I joined in on the fun. We had somehow moved on without Bodjie being the instigator of our joking. He would often start the *biruan* and *asaran* in our *barkada*. Every so often, it would occur to us that he was gone, and silence would descend on us for a while.

One weekend, we were walking to the landfill to scavenge for junk items when we saw a fracas by the roadside. A woman was being helped to safety, and a boy was held down by onlookers and tricycle drivers.

It appeared that the woman had been attacked. Her right arm bled from a bad wound, and her left hand was mangled. The women in the community gathered around her to help, and we heard someone mention they had just called an ambulance for her. The boy the men were holding down must have been responsible for the attack.

The boy struggled frantically against the hold, but he looked vaguely familiar. His eyes were dazed, cloudy, like he was possessed or high. His hospital gown was torn and muddy.

I gasped. It was Boyba. He looked nothing like he used to. His eyes were the deep yellow of dark urine. Blood vessels and sinews showed through his slender neck and shoulders. Loose skin dangled from his belly and waist area. His teeth were rotten, black at the gumline and capped red with the woman's blood. Sores covered his brown skin. He looked like a zombie. He looked just like Vargas.

Jason, Enrico, Laleng, and I stared at one another. We remembered Bodjie and how he had begun his own sudden transformation. My gut lurched; my mouth went dry. What had happened to them? Why were they acting like this? Why were they attacking people?

My mama and papa spoke to me that night after supper.

"Son, do you know that we heard about some of your classmates doing drugs? These addicts are morphing now. Zombies, the police call them. But they mean it literally. Didn't you see these classmates of yours? They attack like zombies!"

I didn't know what to say, so I let Papa talk next.

"Son," he said, "they're growing in number. They move quickly after transforming and pounce on unsuspecting prey. In alleyways and side streets, they drag down children or geriatrics and eat them!"

I was shocked. There was a plague spreading? I thought it was superstition, an urban legend or something.

"People say that they all start as drug addicts, then turn into monsters! Zombies!" my dad said.

"Be careful, son," my mama told me. "Always keep your eyes peeled."

The three of us were sleeping soundly when a ruckus woke us. It came from next door. It was still dark out, maybe 3:30 a.m., and Papa turned on the light. He took his flashlight out to the hallway as Mama warned him to be careful. Papa found Mang Ric on the floor of his room.

Dead.

There was blood on the floor, on the walls. A pool of blood trailed from his abdomen, growing larger as it trickled out of the fist-sized crater where his gut would have been.

His belongings were a mess. His wallet was on the floor. It appeared that some of the contents had been taken: cash, not the picture of his family, not his ID. He was robbed. Papa rushed to the window to see who might have been escaping.

He cried out to Mang Rudy. "It's Dionisio! He's getting away!"

Mang Rudy ran out of his room. He stopped for a moment after seeing Mang Ric on the floor, then performed the sign of the cross before following my dad in pursuit of Dionisio. Crowds outside were in uproar. Papa was waking the neighbors to prevent Dionisio from escaping.

Mama told me to go inside, that she needed to tend to Mang Ric to see if he could be saved. She felt his neck for a pulse, but I knew it was too late.

Mang Ric was working in Manila and living in Tondo's slums so he could send all his earnings to the family in Laguna, especially while Dionisio was attending high school. I wept as Mama stared at me with a helpless expression.

I followed Papa and Mang Rudy in their chase of Dionisio. People all over the community were waking up, peering from their open doors and windows, wondering whether the coast was clear. Some brave men sought to help Papa and Mang Rudy. The folks at the perimeter of Barangay Happyland told them Dionisio hadn't come through there. He must have been hiding somewhere.

I wandered about, looking for Papa, and headed to the landfill. The workers gathered there were also looking for Dionisio. Families from the settlements began signaling the coast was clear in the warehouses, the storage areas, and the pig farms. People were looking under crawlspaces, wondering if Dionisio might be hidden below.

When a loud cry broke across the night, I followed the source of the sound. Papa and Mang Rudy were in the charcoal pits. More loud cries followed. Someone said Dionisio had rounded the corner; he was hiding in the pits or amongst the large stacks of uncooked wood.

Papa and Mang Rudy followed the shrill cry, encircling the perimeter. The fire was raging. Plumes of smoke thickened. The heat was intense, and we didn't think Dionisio would have hidden in the burning coal lest he plunge toward certain death.

I screamed when Dionisio suddenly appeared on top of the cooked batch of charcoal, black as night from ash, lips red like he'd drunk from a fondue of blood, eyes yellow like some kind of monster. He leapt from the top of the heap and landed on my Papa. They rolled along the ground, struggling against one another. The crowds converged. Papa fought Dionisio off with some punches to the face. Dionisio staggered from the blows and struggled to get up on his feet. In a flash, my stomach sank as Dionisio's eyes found me and he darted in my direction. Before I could take a step, his hands were around my neck, tight, as though he planned to break it.

Mang Rudy called out to the others, but Papa raised a hand to stop them. "Leave the poor boy alone, Dionisio. He's innocent!"

Mang Rudy caught up with Papa, and the crowds followed close behind. Dionisio shuffled from foot to foot, like he didn't know what to do now. He was scarecrow-scrawny and covered by thick, black dust from charcoal smoke. He gasped like he was hungry, but…for drugs or…for what? His breath smelled foul, worse than usual. His hands shook, tightening on my throat like he was suffering from tremors; his movements were short and spasmodic, almost like he was in the middle of a seizure. What had happened to him?

From my periphery, I saw him thrust his open mouth at my neck. Fear jolted me into panic as I ducked and darted out of his grasp, quickly running to the safety of Papa's arms. Mang Rudy charged at Dionisio, and the two struggled on the ground until the others came to help. Mang Rudy suddenly cried out in pain. Dionisio had bitten him on the shoulder during the fracas. Some of the men held Dionisio down while others helped Mang Rudy aside.

Papa went to see if Mang Rudy was okay.

"Just a bite," Mang Rudy muttered, grinning to indicate he was fine. But his smile turned to a grimace. "Why would Dionisio bite instead of punch or claw me?"

None of us could understand what was going through Dionisio's mind. First, killing his dad by ripping his guts out, then trying to bite me, then *actually* biting Mang Rudy… Was Dionisio insane?

A zombie?

———— • ————

Mama bandaged Mang Rudy's wounds. He was grateful. "Thank you for your help, Frances," he said. The bite left an angry red mark with some dark bluish liquid discharge. Mama had cleaned the wound with antiseptic and wrapped gauze around it, like how she often nursed Papa's wounds from working at the construction yard, and Mang Rudy promised he would keep an eye on the wound to make sure it was healing properly.

We were interrupted by the morning news on the television. The drug problem was on the rise. Vigilante groups were killing small-time dealers. Armed pushers fought back. Kids doubling as runners were thrown into harsh prisons where they were beaten and gang raped. We imagined Jet and Emerson would have experienced this…had they not turned into those *things*.

Our next objective was to locate Bodjie and convince him to go to rehab. It was his only chance. More and more deaths were resulting from the violence in the streets: addicts and pushers turning into zombies, vigilante groups executing them with automatic weapons. Before I made my way to the landfill to locate Bodjie, I visited Doctor Amorsolo again. He was at the free clinic screening patients for COVID-19 and other diseases. I made an excuse to come, deciding to tell him I needed testing. It wasn't that I wanted to lie, but I needed information.

I fell in line, waiting to be seen. Eventually, I made it into the clinic, and Doctor Amorsolo cheered up big-time when he saw me.

"Mindo, hello," he said. He always smiled at patients, but he beamed especially at the sight of me. He was wonderful with kids.

"I'm okay, Doc," I told him. "I need COVID-19 testing. I have a dry cough."

He said sure, and I sat down. While he prepared the swab kit, I waited for the right time to ask. "About the zombies. The addicts. What has been happening to them?"

He frowned, then raised his chin and looked at me seriously. "Be careful these days, Min. We're seeing an outbreak of horrific proportions. Across Metro Manila, not only here in Tondo. The zombie pandemic is spreading. We're seeing cases rise across the country."

He took a swab sample of my saliva, placed it in the specimen container, then locked it in storage. He faced me once again. "So far, we only know that there is a link between drug addiction and the outbreak."

I couldn't help but be worried. Doctor Amorsolo smiled cautiously.

He gave me a lollipop and told me not to walk alone at night or in tight places where there was no foot traffic.

"Remember what I told you, son, okay?"

I smiled at him, and he mussed my hair. Then I left to meet up with Enrico and Laleng close to the landfill so we could hunt Bodjie down.

Enrico and Laleng were not at the agreed upon spot. I grew worried. Maybe I was late, and they went ahead to scavenge that day? They would always come whenever I asked to meet up, so something was fishy. I didn't assume the worst; it wasn't in my nature. So, I waited for twenty, maybe twenty-five minutes, but after that, I got the itch to leave. I decided to go to the landfill in case their parents had refused to let them out of the house in light of the pandemic.

The last time I spoke to Enrico and Laleng, Jason showed us viral video clips of the supposed zombies attacking people in Manila. Watching the blood-crazed former drug addicts attack victims like wild animals spooked me. The cellphone videos looked like certain evidence of the supposed zombie outbreak. We saw with our own eyes how Boyba and Vargas turned into the same things. But how could drugs do such a thing? It had never happened before.

When I arrived at the landfill, the place was eerily quiet. Where were the scavengers? Had something scared them off? I looked around but couldn't find a soul. That was until I reached a clearing amidst the mountains of garbage and found a group of men hunkered down over something on the ground.

I gasped. They were zombies, stooped over what appeared to be another kid's corpse. I watched them feed, hoisting entrails into the air and feasting on them, splattering blood and guts on the muddy soil and garbage like they were coloring the place with death.

When one of the zombies looked up at me, a shiver ran through my bones. My heart raced so fast, it jolted me. It was Bodjie, with bloody mouth, gore-caked shirt, hands, neck, chin, and fingers.

The body on the ground was Laleng's. I could vaguely make out her features. She'd been devoured alive. There was a hole in her chest and gut to contrast the somber "o" shape of her mouth and deep, visually arresting shock in her eyes.

I ran.

As fast as I could.

I couldn't wrap my mind around what was happening. Laleng was gone, killed by another of my best friends. My cheeks and forehead flushed red with rage, but terror had my legs pumping fast. Were there really so many drug addicts turning into zombies? How were they multiplying so fast?

CHAPTER 6

THE BEGINNING OF THE END

Fires were igniting as I made my way home. Gunshots rang out. I recognized a woman pulling the arm of a teenage girl on the side street—she was the same woman bitten on the hand and arm by Boyba recently. The teenager struggled to break free, but the woman managed to pull the girl's ponytail and take a bite out of her cheek. Blood spurted. The girl's eyeball came loose. A van screeched to a stop, and men rained bullets on the woman.

They shot the girl too.

It was chaos. I didn't know what was happening. I realized they shot the girl because she had been bitten. They showed no remorse for her, spraying her with bullets even though she had been a victim!

I detoured to Enrico's place to see if he was okay. Running through the streets with my mouth open, I took in rapid breaths of air. I bumped into scrambling residents; they looked confused and fearful. When I arrived at Enrico's house, the green gate was open. Bloody handprints marred the walls. I edged up to the door with my heart beating furiously, my mouth dry. When I peeked inside, Enrico's siblings were feeding on their parents, parts of the necks, chest, and breast areas missing chunks of meat and internal organs. The youngest child was suckling on a palpitating heart.

With slow, quiet steps, I retreated. I had to get home, get away from it all.

People were running in all directions like ants during a feeding frenzy. Bodies fell to the ground as the transformed addicts assailed them. Blood spattered. The smell of salty sweat and tears filled the air.

As I dodged and weaved through the chaos, I came upon Laleng's mom. She looked like she was in shock. Dazed. Watching everyone go by like she'd suffered some traumatic event. There was blood on her hands and arms. It looked as though she had successfully survived an attack. I pushed through the frantic crowds toward her, but before I could reach her, a man rushed into her outstretched arms and slammed her to the ground. He bit into her neck, tearing ribbons of flesh free. Blood gushed like a fire sprinkler as he continued to gorge on her neck, this time ripping the larynx and vital blood vessels loose, and the blood became a river. Her hands shook, and her heels drummed against the ground.

The gutters ran crimson.

The man raised his head, eyes wild and baring glistening red teeth. It was Laleng's dad. I ran, fast as I could, in the direction of home.

I ran like the wind, dodging zombies with my small size and quick feet. Didn't stop once during the frantic escape, fleeing those zombies like they were nipping at my heels the whole time. I eventually arrived safely and locked the door behind me, breathing hard, legs shaking. My mama wasn't home yet. When I looked out from the kitchen and service area, chaos was erupting in some of the lower shanties. There was screaming, crying, men reaching for their loved ones, attacking them with their mouths, digging deep into flesh with their teeth, tasting the blood of friends and relatives alike with their black, rotting tongues.

Panic began to set in, and I paced the living room. I needed to know if Mama and Papa were safe. Suddenly, the doorknob rattled. My heart jolted, but seconds later, Mama opened the door. She was terrified. We embraced. Tight. She touched my face, stroked my hair. Said that she was worried about Papa. He was working at the construction site, and all hell was breaking loose.

"It's everywhere, Min. I saw it on the TV at the canteen. We closed, and I came home. It's too dangerous in the streets. What about your papa? What do we do?"

Tears streamed down our faces. I knew Mama felt as helpless as I did.

"We'll stay here. Let's barricade the door. Quickly!"

I grabbed a chair and jammed it under the door handle. Then I helped my mama push a table over to the door to barricade it closed.

We jumped back when a scream sounded just outside. There were sounds of footsteps. More screams. Some for help. Others in fear, pain. We heard chairs and tables making impact, splintering, bodies thudding against walls, the crack of skulls fracturing, revealing soft, pulpy brain matter: food for the new gods.

Mama and I fell to the floor, sitting in a corner of the day room. We held each other tightly, and she continued to stroke my hair.

She cried softly while repeating Papa's name. "Josel. Josel. Josel..."

An hour later, the terrifying sounds had not ceased. Police were running up and down the streets, firing at the zombies. Gunshots tore loose from passing vehicles. Bullets tore through bodies. Tires screeched in the distance; other times, very close. Residents fell from shanties on the second and third level into the bay. The polluted, black waters didn't show a tiny hint of red even after many bodies plummeted into its depths.

The doorknob rattled. A muffled scream tore loose.

"Frances, Min, this is Josel!" the voice said. "Open the door!"

Mama immediately raced to the door. She shoved the table away and dislodged the chair. Papa opened it. He was wounded at the arm and shoulder. His shirt was bloody, and he was shaking. We helped him inside and let him rest on the floor. Then we barricaded the door again.

"Who did this to you, Josel? Did those monsters attack you?" Mama said.

"It was Rudy! Do you remember what happened to him? He was bitten by Dionisio. He was working with me at the construction site. Then he changed. He turned into one of those things!" Fear was sketched on Papa's face. "He's a zombie now."

Mama bandaged Papa's arm and shoulder with some gauze while I fetched a glass of water for him.

He didn't stop shaking. Mama said that he might have an infection. We needed to take him to a hospital, but the streets were dangerous. We decided to stay, and eventually Papa quieted down. He closed his eyes and rested. Mama and I watched him. Occasionally, he fidgeted, like the tail end of a seizure. Or maybe that a more serious convulsion was about to happen.

Mama looked out of our service area. More women and children from the shanties overlooking the bay fell into the water, screaming before making impact. They struggled to swim in the trenches of waste and bodies. The embankment full of trash held their arms and legs down. Survivors of the fall would simply get stuck and drown.

Some shanties were on fire. Mama looked at me, worriedly. "The fires, *anak*. They will spread to our community. All the shanties will burn down tonight. If not tonight, tomorrow."

I had an idea. It was worth a try. "*Inay*, we have to get you and Papa to a shelter. There's a place I know at the landfill. After I take you there, I'll try to look for supplies for us. Food and water. Antibiotics for Papa."

Mama couldn't look at me at first, but she finally did and nodded. "I can't believe how brave you are," she said. Tears streamed down her cheeks while she held my head against hers, mumbling a prayer.

"Your papa might not last the night here. His wound is infected. The police are killing everyone. Even the wounded. I don't understand it. We need to take him to shelter and get him medicine."

We let Papa rest a little longer, then we woke him. His eyes were yellowish. His veins started darkening, popping out. His fingernails looked bruised.

Mama and I refused to think he was headed for the worst-case scenario, that he was going to end up like those zombies. Those things. They weren't the slow, lurching zombies in movies. These were like the ones in *Train to Busan*. This wave brought forth a new breed: as quick and adept as humans, as hungry as starving, wild animals.

I refused to believe Papa would give in. Despite the physical signs, he was still quiet, still human. He looked at me with his yellow eyes and smiled reassuringly. He was still my papa. Not a beast.

I grabbed his short sword, his *itak*, from the service area, then carefully opened the door and peered down the long passageway. Silence and darkness greeted us. I told Mama we had to be quiet, and we helped Papa out and eventually reached the staircase. It looked as though the violence had died down somewhat since police began shooting anyone suspicious in the area. Fires had burned down some shanties, and smoke carpeted the air. Sacks of garbage were burning. Beside homes, drums filled with recycled products melted in the fire and sent toxic smoke everywhere. We muffled our coughing as best we could.

We climbed down and sped through the dark, smoky air like we had wings. Gave it every ounce of effort, fleet-footed and stealthy, as we made our way down the street toward the landfill on the fringes of Barangay Happyland.

The scavengers loitering or taking the route to and from the landfill were noticeably absent. Occasionally, we heard shouts, screams for help.

We didn't stop. When a woman burst out of nowhere and clung onto my mama's arm, screaming, Mama panicked. She screamed, "Mindo!"

I came to her aid. The assailant had been bitten in multiple areas. Her eyes were deep yellow, and veins throbbed blue and black. "Let go of my mom!" I yelled, and swung the blade to slice the woman's arm, cutting it at the wrist.

The woman howled as blood shot out of her severed arm. My mama shook the woman's hand free, and I promptly returned to Papa's side, supporting him by the shoulder as Mama took his other side.

Off we went, walking briskly, fending off tears and trying to be brave.

———————————

The entrance of the landfill was flanked by two steel drums filled with lit garbage, smoke rising high like pillars. The landfill was aglow with several lit drums. In the shanties among the trash, eyes peered out of the dark, smudged windows. They watched for every sign of movement in the landfill, fearing the armies of undead. These survivors had barricaded their houses as we had done.

The residents had likely lit up the garbage bins to see each other's faces. One could tell zombie from normal human by a simple look at the face and body: the dark yellow fingernails, the blue and black veins, the yellow corneas, the pupils of the eyes whitening and clouding like they had dilated to twice the usual size, the fingers that retracted to make clawing gestures.

I supported Papa's weight from my side the best I could. Mama did as well, even if she struggled to keep up. We had to hurry over to the trap door before more of the zombies reached the landfill. So far, one of the worst places on Earth to live remained one of the safest.

We were careful not to trip over loose trash, slowing to get a solid footing, prioritizing getting Papa safely up the slope to the burrow. We reached the spot on the slope where the trap door was located, and I asked Mama to let Papa sit on the mound while I made sure the hole was vacant. While Papa sat and relaxed his wounded shoulder, I opened the trap door and got ready to use my *itak*.

Nothing. I waited a few seconds, summoning my nerve before taking a peek. The hole was empty. Elated, I gestured for Mama to get down the ladder first so I could help Papa down.

When Mama reached the bottom, she held her arms open for Papa, who climbed down very carefully, nursing his wounded shoulder. He was weakening, but I did my best to support his weight so Mama could simply help him down. We heaved a big sigh of relief when he finally made it. Mama made him rest on the ground while she tended to his bloody bandages.

I crept close to them and whispered, "I'll fetch food, water, and medicine. Stay here. Don't leave."

Papa smiled at me. Beads of sweat covered his forehead, and his temperature was rising. He held my arm gently as if to thank me. I left his *itak* by his side for protection.

Papa handed the *itak* to Mama, indicating that she would have to use it in case he would cross over. She looked at it but didn't take it.

Mama turned to face me, tears in her eyes. "God be with you, *anak*. Please come back to us, son. Be very careful out there."

<hr />

I climbed the staircase and exited the room, shutting the trap door before covering it up with some loose trash so no one would see it.

With my parents safe, I quickly made my way out of the landfill to search through the streets of Tondo again. When I first passed the place where the free clinic was stopped, the truck wasn't there. Owing to the violence and the time of day, I hadn't pinned my hopes on it anyway, so I decided to look for a pharmacy instead. With no money, if the pharmacy was open I'd have to beg for the medicine or promise to pay it back somehow. If they were closed, I was committed to breaking and entering because Papa's life was on the line.

I thought about getting him to a hospital, but the nearest one was some distance away, and the roads in Tondo were filled with vehicles due to the riots. People ran this way and that in the shadows, scurrying feet that had my skin crawling. You never knew which ones were zombies. I felt fairly certain the zombies were opportunistic; they waited for slower prey, not those who could easily outrun them. I figured they would wait for people too defeated to fight for survival, possibly insane with grief after the deaths of loved ones. Turned out I was wrong. These zombies were frantic: their arms and legs jerked and twitched, their movements were spasmodic, and even if they reminded me of the scavenger underneath the trap door in the landfill who was overdosing on *shabu*, these zombies chased after prey, using numbers to overwhelm their victims.

There was little choice but to try to get help from the police. I tried to approach one policeman, but he suddenly pointed his gun at me. I shook my head to say I was innocent and raised my hands.

My eyes flew wide. He was signaling to his fellow policemen that he was going to open fire.

I jumped into a ditch just as he did. The bullets sprayed the ground where I'd stood just seconds ago, causing a ringing in my ears. I crawled frantically down the ditch and made my way into a drainage port. The flowing water stank of raw sewage. It splashed into my mouth, entered my nostrils. I had no choice but to crawl in it for several meters until I reached an opening in the drainage site. Then I dragged myself out.

Clusters of decaying matter fell from my cheeks, my eyelashes, and my ears when I wiped my face, but I had to keep moving so the cops would not catch me.

I ran through the dark streets. Others ran too. There was screaming, crying. Shrieks and howls. Sirens wailed. Gunshots erupted. I couldn't believe what was happening. Zombies were coming out of nowhere, and the rest of us were being exterminated by the police. They didn't know who was safe from infection. They were scared themselves; you could see it in their faces. They were shooting anyone and everyone.

I needed help, and tried to find a vehicle to transport Papa, so I stopped a motorcyclist from taking off. "Please help us," I said. "My dad is sick."

The cyclist swatted my outstretched hands away. Then he drove straight into a car plowing through people in oncoming traffic.

A pedicab driver was busily pedaling down a side street, hurrying to get away from the zombies. I blocked his way and asked him to help me. "Help us! Please!" I repeated, just as I had the first time. He waved me off frantically, but I refused to budge. Suddenly, however, a woman darted out of nowhere and attacked the pedicab driver. Her jaw unhinged and she bit into his neck, tearing into the side of his head, leaving shreds of loose meat exposing his spine.

I backpedaled as the pedicab driver tried pushing her off, but soon more zombies converged on him. There was nothing I could do but run. I bumped into another fleeing resident and fell to the ground. Stunned, I sat there, half-expecting zombies to attack or crowd me. However, I was soon up on my feet and running once more. The pharmacy was only a short distance away. I had to make it. Papa needed antibiotics and antiseptics for his wound.

Running down chaotic streets, past burning homes with screams tearing through the night, I made it safely to the neighborhood pharmacy to find the steel door chained and padlocked. I searched for something to smash the padlock but couldn't find anything that would help. I tried to wrench the padlock free with my hands, but it was impossible. There was no access to the pharmacy, no access to a vehicle to take Papa to the hospital. Defeated, I retreated to a corner where there were food stalls and decided to loot the place for any provisions.

Others had gotten there first, but there was bread left over in a hamburger stall. It was slightly moldy, likely expired—throwaway inventory. I took it. Then, I found a half-empty bottle of water with the cap on inside a nearby trash can. I undid the cap, smelled the water, and judged it safe. My next objective was to see if I could hijack a motorcycle, and after a frantic search, I found one parked deep in the market, beyond the first and second row of empty food stalls. "Yes!"

I eased it from under its covers and kickstarted it, relieved that things were finally turning my way. I hightailed it to the landfill with my supply of food and water.

Zipping through roads filled with zombies that were feeding on people, I weaved through traffic on the narrow streets. Shared the roads with police patrol cars dropping off officers into the frontlines, military vehicles that were shooting at zombies and innocent civilians alike. Gunshots ricocheted off the ground nearby, coming so close I could almost feel the rush of wind. I skidded around turns as I sped through the violence, taking blind turns left and right as I regained my bearings after drifting off-course.

Still, I realized how far away from the landfill I was, having to zigzag around stopped traffic in C.M. Recto Avenue, threading between sidewalks and parked cars beside universities and large networks of small stores. Everywhere, cars slammed into rear fenders. Large trucks capsized after skidding against the rails. People ran and screamed and shoved others out of their way in frantic panic. It was easy enough to see the zombies chasing the slower civilians, the wounded. Easy prey.

I sped all the way to Tutuban Center Mall. Chaos unfolded into more chaos. Tents of *tiangges* were torn to shreds—zombies must have been underneath them, attacking the vendors. Products hanging from steel wire fences fell onto the sidewalks with a clatter, only adding to the cacophony of a dying district. People fleeing the zombies ran over these items, tripped and fell. The rest: game over.

The buildings were like high-rise prisons. The entrances were under siege, and there was no other way out. Bodies fell from top-floor windows, smashing on the ground in front of me. Screams pierced the air. High-pitched wails never seemed to cease. Windows shattered into millions of tiny shards; floods of people were attacked coming out of the elevators in lobbies. People climbed out of windows and jumped to their deaths. I just *knew* the zombies were rampaging down hallways and building entrances, hunting down the uninfected.

During my time escaping the outbreak of chaos, I had seen a news segment broadcasting coverage nationwide. A reporter could be seen, describing the carnage. "The violence is spreading throughout the country. The zombie outbreak is at its hilt. The same horrors in Manila can be found in the provinces. Corpses getting up from the roadsides in small towns. Zombies chasing helpless people. Pandemonium." Where would I escape to? Tondo was home, and it was all I ever really knew.

When I made it to Radial Road R-10, I weaved through traffic, dodging people and zombies and police alike until I reached Barangay Happyland. At the landfill, I negotiated the loose trash with my bike, slowly dredging old plastic cups and bags, plastic forks and spoons.

I finally made it to where I had left Mama and Papa, parked the bike, and opened the trap door. My parents were huddled in a corner, shielding their eyes with their arms. They appeared to be afraid of the light.

"Mama, Papa, I'm here now."

Something was wrong. I felt it in my gut.

They writhed in the shadows, hid in the corner, making clawed gestures with their hands. I feared the worst, but refused to believe it. Something inside me broke into tiny bits of pieces. I wanted to climb down, run into their arms, embrace them both, and allow them to turn me into a zombie…just like them.

A second ticked by. Another. Then they lunged forward, scrabbling on hands and knees. Survival instinct kicked in, and I clambered up, slammed the trap door, and covered it under garbage, leaving the ventilation hole free so they could breathe.

Their growls and moans oozed past the barricade. They were hungry, ravenous for blood and meat.

I backed up, each step away from them painful yet steeling my resolve. I'd get help from an ambulance. Doctors would know how to treat Mama and Papa, they *had* to. Leaving them there to get help sapped all my courage. What if the entire city was engulfed in flames, and no one would help? I jumped back on my motorcycle and sped toward the exit.

The shanties guarding the entrance to the landfill were under siege. Other scavenger-zombies were breaking into the ramshackle dwellings, attacking the families inside. Screams tore through the night. The zombie scavengers were ten-times hungrier and scarier than others living in better slum areas. They groaned like their bellies were on fire. They raked flesh with their long, gore-caked fingernails. They were barbarity and carnage incarnate—mauling faces beyond recognition, ripping viscera from soft flesh, snapping bones and wrenching limbs free.

I sped past them, only to find one more zombie waiting for me on the road back to the city.

Bodjie.

I did not want to confront Bodjie.

Being on a motorcycle meant I could pass him quickly. However, the road was narrow. Worse, behind me, the landfill and the scavengers-turned-zombies awaited.

Bodjie had a look of recognition on his face. It was also clear he wanted to orient me with his language of suffering—to become a zombie just like him...or a snack.

Sure, we had been friends once. But as my parents showed me, the transformation that took place after infection rendered him and the others indiscriminating toward taste.

I tried hard to think of the narrow two-lane road ahead and the chances of slipping past Bodjie. However, he stood in the middle of the lanes, anchored to the ground like he wasn't about to let supper escape.

I didn't like my chances of passing him on either side, so I decided to charge right at him. *So much for not confronting him.* I revved the engine and allowed the back wheel to slide sideways. Then, I stepped on the gas and shot through the dark, smoky air straight at Bodjie.

He didn't react at all. He absorbed the blow and hammered me and the top of the bike like a cannonball.

I flew off the seat and slammed onto my back as the bike skidded forward. It landed on its side before the engine cut out. My head was spinning as I sat up and scanned the surroundings. Smoke rose into the night. Everywhere, fires raged. Across the landfill, the burning rubbish sent toxic smoke and chemicals into my lungs. The other scavenger-zombies groaned, still impossibly hungry—

Shooting to my feet, I spun to find Bodjie suddenly lunging forward. I stumbled back, and he fell at my feet, grabbing for me as I scampered back and dodged his grasp.

I ran for the bike, hefted it up, and tried kicking the ignition over and over, but it wouldn't start.

Bodjie was struggling to get up as I continued to desperately kickstart the bike, but his foot was facing the wrong way. I watched on, horrified, as he twisted it back into place with a crack, then did the same to his dislocated shoulder, fixing them without feeling a thing. He didn't scream in pain or even let out a muffled cry. He just twisted his limbs like it was no big deal.

I had to run, but I gave the motorcycle one last kick, and it churned back to life. The engine coughed, hissed, and blew smoke, but I cranked it up with one yank of the handles before I leapt onto the seat and sped away to the sound of Bodjie's howls.

———— • ————

Adrenaline fueled my escape, and I weaved past traffic accidents, dodging other motorcycles that ran counterflow to my mission—find a hospital and a doctor to help Mama and Papa, maybe even Bodjie.

The scene at Tondo General Hospital was a firestorm, a slaughter. It was something straight out of the Book of Revelation.

Fire trucks pumped water to the top floors of the building where burning bodies fell from balconies and windows and slammed against the ground. Some broke apart on impact, their insides still sizzling. Others moved. They kicked, spasmed, then rose to their haunches, bones jutting at unnatural angles, and attacked policemen and firefighters.

Some patients on the top floor were jumping from the windows to escape fire, some to escape the zombies, who were attacking the elderly, children, anyone they could get their hands and teeth on. The zombies stripped meat from emaciated limbs. They bit into lactating breasts. Some mauled small faces and gouged eyeballs with claw-like fingers. Blood sprayed the outer walls of the hospital below—a bloody mural painted from the five floors of the building. Every window leaked blood, and entrails dangled from them like a butcher's shop. Hands scooped brain tissue from fractured skulls, shoving the meat into hungry mouths. Gore-stained lips dripped soft viscera, and they moaned as though they were chanting some moribund mantra. It was like the mythical beast of rebellion had sent his minion to massacre the most ill of Tondo.

It was Armageddon.

Security and staff did their best to fight the surge of zombie infection from the lower floors. They barricaded hallways, quarantined departments. Fought the influx of zombies seeking entry through broken windows by smashing at their heads with folded chairs or anything that came to hand—nightsticks, fire extinguishers—whatever they needed to prevent getting bitten. They sprayed chemical sanitizers into the zombies' eyes, temporarily stunning them.

From the windows, I saw the ill rising from beds, newly transformed. Pictured them raging through the hallways, ravenous, seeking victims, drawing fresh blood from incapacitated patients or tired nurses, most of the latter having battled similar zombies all night.

Gunshots fired from the entrance. Flashes of light flickered throughout the hospital. Fluorescent bulbs blew up in several rooms, in several wards, sending sparks raining down, lighting small fires amidst the gloom. The nurses and staff were waging a losing war. Their expressions foretold doom.

The zombies multiplied. Some fell to the street, heads mashed to a pulp. They did not care for survival, driven only by the relentless urge to feed.

There was no hope in bringing Mama and Papa to safety here or at any other hospital, but how could I walk away from my parents? How could I not do something? I thought about leaving them in the underground room until the government found a cure. But where would I go? No place was safe.

Another burning body plummeted to the ground. It writhed, kicked like Frankenstein's monster after being given a shot of life. When the small fires on the man's lab coat died, after he spasmed uncontrollably on the pavement, he rose jerkily to his feet and looked at me. It took a moment, but then my gut dropped.

Doctor Amorsolo.

All gray skin and shriveled flesh, burnt hair, tattered lab coat charred at the ends, yellow eyes looking famished. He stared straight into my eyes and raced past firefighters, policemen, and soldiers, charging toward me.

I gunned the engine and left him, my doctor, my friend, behind.

CHAPTER 7

ESCAPE

I raced away from Tondo General Hospital and crossed the Radial Road R-10 back to Barangay Happyland.

Happyland was burning.

I was back to where it all began.

Recall: the inferno was eating up Happyland and the bodies started piling. Zombies were multiplying, feasting on survivors taking to the streets.

A sign consisting of an interlaced set of steel grids forming the letters *Welcome to Barangay Happyland* greeted visitors with a hellish afterglow. Smoke and fire rose into the night as old rubber tires, plastic recyclables, plywood, clothing, *yero*, and dead flesh burned like midnight oil for the hopeless. The sign was like an angel's halo—an angel burning in hell!

I navigated my motorcycle into the inner reaches of the slum, heading to the landfill to say goodbye to Mama and Papa. What else was I going to do for them? I would have to wait until a cure was created and revisit them one day. Or I would let them die of hunger in the underground shelter instead of letting them kill someone else. It was the only way. I couldn't let them hurt anyone, and I knew they would not want to hurt anyone either.

The wheels dredged burnt plastic and mud until I hit a clear path and then headed toward the landfill where I had faced off with Bodjie. One more time around the sun with my old friend perhaps.

He was not there. Drums of lit rubbish burned like large votive candles paying homage to the thousands of dead. I glanced at the shanties closest to the landfills to find the residents eviscerated, whole sections of their anatomy missing, the leftovers unrecognizable after the brutal carnage.

I moved along, and found Mama and Papa's hiding place amidst the loose garbage. I peered into the ventilation hole and saw no movement. "Mama, Papa, *paalam po*. Goodbye," I said, crying like an infant. I sat there for a while, unable to leave them despite knowing that perhaps I was leaving for good. Who knew what could be done to save Tondo's population?

A growl broke through my sobs. Then another. I had woken my parents, and they stretched clawed fingers up for the ventilation hole, trying to reach me before climbing up the ladder. They tried pushing the door open, and it thumped back into place, but their hunger meant they would not stop. I staggered to my feet and ran to the motorbike as the door broke free.

Up came Mama and Papa, fully transformed zombies.

The ground was muddy and soft as I dragged the motorcycle to a clear patch of ground. I couldn't afford to be impeded by debris, to fall and lose this advantage I had. However, the bike became a hindrance; I couldn't get on and take off just yet.

Death was everywhere, stripping Happyland's bones clean. The charcoal pits smoldered, but there were no more workers; the slow-cooked wood had been engulfed by rapidly growing embers. The pig farms were quiet; gone was the tireless sound of pigs squealing. Gone, too, were the basketball courts, wooden clapboards all burned to cinders, hoops crumbled on the ground. The settlements were devoured by flames, concrete structures like charred skeletons. Hung drapes fanned in the wind like lit banana leaves in the provinces. The embankment stretching Manila Bay was deserted; only corpses washed up along the rocks amid old tires and trash.

Mama and Papa were nipping at my heels. I had to get to clear ground before mounting my bike or I would never escape.

Gunshots suddenly tore through the night, and I instinctively ducked. I heard the meaty thud of bullets tearing through flesh. Ahead, a policeman was aiming his gun at me, but it took a moment to realize he had actually fired at targets behind me. *Mama… Papa…*

I turned around. Mama and Papa's bodies were splayed on the ground. "Run, kid!" the policeman yelled. I panicked, but I raced over to my parents instead. Dropping to my knees, I covered my mouth and sobbed when I saw their faces—still as sunrise hovering over the bay, peaceful and joyful like the photos on our walls. Grief washed over me, and I drowned in it even though I knew they were free now. I whispered a prayer. *Please protect my parents, Lord. Rest in peace po, Mama and Papa.*

I hesitated before leaving. I wanted to bury them, but knew that doing so would simply jeopardize my chances of escaping. Mama and Papa would want me to be safe, to live.

More gunshots resounded, then a scream; it sounded like the policeman. I stumbled to my motorcycle, negotiated the muddy road, and crossed the Radial Road R-10 via the nearest intersection to the other side of Barangay Happyland. R-10 was backed up with bumper-to-bumper traffic, and hordes of zombies were picking and choosing motorists stranded on the road. An all-you-can-eat buffet.

The sight was gruesome. Every major building was ablaze. Police and the military were outnumbered. Helicopters dropped water over buildings, mainly shelters… The same shelters were overwhelmed by the number of residents turning into zombies. It was just like the hospital. From kids with small bite wounds to adults who did not disclose getting bitten. Crowded residential areas were under siege, the tight spaces and side streets turning bloody. There was no chance to flee. Zombies were climbing walls and gates, forcing their way into homes, heads and shoulders smashing into wooden doors, splintering the flimsy protection.

I took the Vitas Bridge over what would have been Bodjie's home above the Estero de la Vitas. The homes under the bridge had collapsed into the polluted water, and bodies had washed up along the mountains of trash by the embankments. Among them, I spotted Bodjie's alcoholic father, fed on by Bodjie's younger siblings.

As the past collided with the presnt, I played tag with the zombies for three days and two nights, sleeping with one eye open in empty houses, always moving on the morning after supplies were gone. I had to find some place safer; either that, or someone who had made it out alive through all of this. I thought of where. Where else?

School. It was the only place I could think of to look for help. Maybe the teachers had been organizing rescues.

When I arrived at Amado V. Hernandez Elementary, the school building was steeped in shadow and quiet. The gate was open, but I didn't trust that it was safe inside. Zombies could have been hunting for survivors. Or they could have been waiting inside in ambush.

Movement flashed across my peripheral vision, and I turned, ready to flee. However, I knew that face. It was Jason, panic-stricken, unsure whether to fight me or flee.

"Jason," I cried out. "Is that you?"

"Yes, Min. It's Jason!"

I rushed over to the school's entrance and inspected him for bite marks or obvious wounds. Jason did the same to me. When I determined he was scratch-less and bite-free, I hugged him, relieved. I couldn't believe someone had survived.

"They're all dead. Either that, or they're zombies now!" I told him.

"Where do we go, Min? My family was eaten alive by my father!" He wept on my shoulder, and I kept an eye out for any zombies as I consoled him as best I could.

"*Huwag kang mag-alala*. Don't worry," I said. "We'll find a place to hide."

"Where?"

I knew where.

"Come on. To the construction site. Do you still remember where?"

———— ◦ ————

We stashed my bike near campus and walked to the nearby construction site. Jason held tight to my arm, and I signaled whether the coast was clear, whether to caution or stop. He heeded my commands. Every so often, screams erupted, so we halted. We watched for movement inside cars that had smashed into electric posts, from bodies sprawled across the front lawns and the roadsides. Occasionally, survivors ran out of houses, bitten in places where family members had attacked them. We watched some bodies on the sidewalk spasm to life as new zombies. They walked erect again, bestowed with new life. They sniffed at the air for fresh blood, not carrion, and it seemed they could tell which was which. We ran, but carefully, staying close, not leaving the other behind. When the coast was clear, we ducked beneath the steel fence of the construction yard and squeezed through the hole in the wall.

The site was deserted, so we sighed in relief. Jason reached into his bag for a flashlight. I stopped him from turning it on. "Not yet," I told him. "Let's look around."

The farther inside the construction site we probed, the safer and more secluded we felt. We found our spot: the cistern where I'd once been trapped when we all played hide-and-seek what seemed like life-times ago.

This time, Jason and I were opening the manhole cover by ourselves.

"*Sige.* Come on. Let's hide until the zombie unrest dies down."

We opened the manhole cover and peeked inside, finding nothing, no one, not even rats. We went in.

The sound of the slab of steel clinking back into place above us was like music. We were safe.

I told Jason, "Let's get food and supplies once we're hungry."

He nodded, wiped his eyes, then took out his flashlight. He turned it on and did his monster face.

Jack en poy
Hale, hale hoy
Sino matalo, siyang unggoy!

"Not funny!" I told him. Then we both laughed.

It did not last, and Jason was soon crying again.

It was dark and slimy inside this place, but it was safe. I held him by the shoulder, and he leaned his head against mine, softly weeping with me until dawn.

Jason turned his flashlight on and checked his watch. Several hours had passed and it was early morning. We had slept maybe two, three hours, but we were still exhausted. Adrenaline kicked in again because those things were still out there. The horrors of last night stayed with us; it was most likely never leaving. I gestured to Jason that we needed to check whether the coast was clear outside. We slowly, carefully, quietly, raised the lid until it came free. We slid the cover open. Its grating sound briefly rattled our nerves.

Jason craned his neck and peeked through the hole while I held the lid up. "No zombies," he whispered.

We were fortunate. Light had broken, yet the sky was the color of ash. Smoke rose into the bleak sky—a holocaust dawn.

"I have a plan," I said, and we closed the lid again.

Jason turned the flashlight on and nodded at me to explain.

"Jason, I'll get food and water, okay? Stay here. So you'll be safe."

His eyes narrowed with worry, and he was on the verge of tears again. "Don't leave me. Can we just stay here instead?"

I patted him on the shoulder and gave him a reassuring smile. "We need to eat. We might get separated if we're chased by those things. I'll be back. I promise."

Jason nodded and followed me to raise the lid again. I looked out, ensuring the coast was clear before sliding through and closing the lid once more. The breeze brought with it the smell of an electrical fire, burning steel, burning garbage. I carefully made my way through drainage ports on the construction site, double-checking ahead before crawling through. I finally reached the hole in the wall and squeezed out.

———————

The aftermath of the warzone hit me like a punch to the gut. Smashed cars littered the road, bent metal and shattered glass pooling around them. Motorcycles sprawled across front lawns, some bent and twisted while others looked like they were just waiting to be picked up by their owners. Chunks of human remains were piled upon sidewalks like a meat market. Blood washed the streets.

Smoke still rose from buildings and homes. Intense heat radiated from nearby infernos. Explosions burst out everywhere. There was so much chaos, and so much death.

Helicopters circled overhead, but I remembered the policeman who opened fire at me and decided they wouldn't help. I didn't know where the zombies had gone. Besides the sound of propellers, it was quiet; no one was screaming, so I doubted whether there were many survivors left. I tiptoed to a house with an open gate. We needed food. Maybe canned goods. Anything. Water from a pitcher in the refrigerator, even if it was no longer cold.

I peered past the gate. The house looked quiet. A car was parked in the driveway, and I edged up to it. There was no blood inside, not on the seats nor the steering wheel. The house looked untouched by the zombies. An oasis within the riots. Potted plants gave the property a touch of serenity. Nothing moved behind the windows, and the front door and walls were spotless. I turned the knob. The door opened.

Perhaps the residents had escaped and were evacuated by the police. So I took a chance. I entered the small living room. The TV was on: a news program showing footage of the slaughter at the Shrine of the Santo Nino de Tondo. Even the church hadn't been spared. On the screen was Jet, Emerson, and other detention-center youths, transformed into blood-thirsty zombies, stampeding through the doors and feasting on devotees. I couldn't watch.

Keeping quiet, I tiptoed to the dining room. Nothing was toppled over, nothing looked out of place. In the kitchen, I peered through the window to the back yard. Quiet there too. The back door behind me was closed. But the nearby refrigerator called all my attention. I opened it quietly and took out a pitcher of water and some bread when noises broke out from behind the back door.

Fingernails scratched at it. Moaning.

I jumped. Made a run for it.

The door sprang open. Out came the maid, a zombie.

I hugged the bread and water pitcher to me and raced back through the house and out the gate, adrenaline fueling my legs, fear fueling my determination to survive. The zombie lost the foot race. I made sure she wasn't on my tail when I finally turned the corner toward the construction site. After a quick check to make sure the coast was clear, I ducked under the steel fence and parted the long stalks of grass before entering the hole in the wall.

I negotiated the drainage ports on the site pretty well for a hungry, dehydrated kid, then was finally at the manhole cover.

The stale bread and warm water were the best breakfast Jason and I had ever had.

———— ♦ ————

By the afternoon, I was out of the manhole, crawling the drainage ports like a SWAT team member to the hole in the wall.

Nothing moved outside. From shadow to shadow, I crept close to walls or ducked behind cars. I peeked into the vehicles but there were no zombies, just human remains plopped on the seats, missing organs or hefty sections of their anatomy. Some scenes were bloodier than others.

A block away I found a store with bars on the windows. The door was padlocked. There were no zombies inside.

While I didn't want to make noise, didn't want to attract any zombies, we needed food. We needed water. I scrounged a lead pipe from a pile of junk nearby and struck the padlock. Hard. The sound made me jump, and I ducked beneath a car and waited, my heart hammering in my chest, sure that zombies were headed my way. I counted to a hundred…two hundred…three. When I reached four hundred and no zombies had come for me, I went back to the door.

Desperate now, I hit the padlock repeatedly until it finally came loose. After making sure the street was clear, I eased open the door, checking for movement. It was blessedly still.

Time to loot the store. I grabbed snacks and soda bottles, bread and water, shoving them into a plastic bag. Behind the counter, I found bandages and antiseptic, and shoved them into my stash.

Back at the front door, I peeked outside. All was still quiet. I closed the door behind me; I could always come back for more supplies when we needed. Taking the same route back, I kept the iron bar with me. I still had the knife in my pocket, but the iron bar gave me reach, kept me farther away from clawing hands and gnashing teeth. I checked around corners to make sure I wouldn't run into any zombies, but at the last corner before reaching the construction site, I caught a glimpse of two kids coming from the direction of the school.

It couldn't be.

It was Bodjie and Enrico, limping while lumbering forward. Their legs appeared broken; they hobbled but managed to walk. Their arms hung limp at their sides, like puppets without strings.

I ducked through the hole and quickly made my way through the obstacles on site. I knocked on the lid and called out to Jason, who slid the cover open. At first, his eyes widened with excitement when he spotted the stash. Then his expression changed when he saw the look on my face.

"They're coming," I said. "Close the lid. Hopefully, they don't know we're here."

"Who's 'they'?" Jason asked.

For a moment, I couldn't speak.

"Who?" he asked again.

"Bodjie and Enrico. They're zombies. They're headed here from the direction of the school."

We kept quiet inside the cistern. We explored the tunnel leading to the far side of the drainage port; there were rusty iron bars marking the dead-end. I took a knife from my pocket and dug into the decayed cement so we could pull the iron bars free. The rushing sewage below flowed like a river of black blood. While I chipped away at the bars, Jason listened for Bodjie and Enrico.

Jason was shivering. He didn't want to let go of my arm. For several seconds, we chipped away, and despite carving out a great deal of debris supporting the structure, the iron bars held firm. We tried pushing it, but it wouldn't budge. We were careful not to make any noise. Jason stared at the manhole cover with dread.

After five minutes passed, all was still quiet. Maybe Bodjie and Enrico hadn't come this way. Jason went to check, and when he raised the lid, he nearly dropped it in a panic. "I saw them," he said, rushing over. "They were in the area. They look like they're leaving now."

I hesitated. Then I went right back to digging us out of the tunnel. The cement had given way to dirt, and I increased my efforts.

"What's wrong?" Jason asked.

"Help me. Quickly! Quickly!" We had yet to dig enough dirt to dislodge the structure when the steel plate began sliding open.

"Min! Faster!" Jason said.

I dropped the dull knife and frantically dug with my hands. Next, I pushed at the iron bars, and they gave way, but only slightly. I tried kicking it loose, but it only budged a little.

Bodjie appeared, groaning like the specter of a wild beast. He reached out with his clawed hands, his feeble, thin arms. The look in his eyes spoke only of hunger. He wasn't human. He wasn't feeding on crops. He delighted in the hunt for fresh meat. Wanted to tear into our chests, excise our beating hearts.

He grabbed Jason, who tried to fight free. I continued kicking at the iron bars until it came loose.

"Jason! Come on!" I grabbed his hand, but Bodjie and Enrico descended on him, pulled him away.

"Min!" he called out as they both held him down and took mouthfuls of flesh and blood. "Min!"

It was too late. They would either turn him into a zombie or devour most of him. I closed my eyes and held my breath. *I'm sorry, Jason.*

I jumped into the flowing river of sewage.

———— ⊳ ⊲ ————

I hurtled through the dark drainage tunnels beneath Tondo, swallowing rot and filth, feces and waste. It swamped my mouth, my nostrils, and my ears. My eyes stung, and I was sure I could feel parasites wiggling past my eyeballs. I ricocheted down muddy walls, large masses of trash and shit clinging to my body. Trying to keep my head above the river of sewage was getting harder and harder, each gasp of filthy air churning my stomach. I sank beneath the surface but clawed my back to that filthy air. I was tired. So tired. My arms felt leaden, and I could barely move my legs. It would be so much easier to just close my eyes and sink—

Light.

Harsh and blinding.

I hit the water hard. Sank. But this wasn't the sludge of the sewer pipe, this was the bay. I struggled to the surface, and was washed up along the rocks, the raw sewage flowing into the muddy banks and tainting the water. I crawled farther up the rocks, finding a nook that looked safe enough and collapsing into it, surrendering to the darkness that followed.

———— ⊳ ⊲ ————

Nausea had me lurch to waking, and I rolled onto my side and threw up. Purged my stomach of what I could, and tried to forget the taste that lingered on my tongue.

Bodies had washed up along the rocks. The residents of Barangay Happyland who had fallen from their homes into the bay during the zombie riots. The bodies were rotting, eyeballs were missing, so, too, their tongues. Their chests had been ripped open, broken ribs jutting toward the sky. Entrails snaked from their abdomens, and I turned away from the mess at their pelvic areas.

With a groan, I pushed to a crouch. Every muscle aching. There were cargo vessels in the nearby port, and I made those my next target. Maybe it was the only safe place. Anywhere but Tondo. The streets were flooded with stranded cars. Remnants of vehicular accidents marred intersections. Huge pile-ups sent residual smoke rising from highways. Somewhere, in gaps between cars or in the rooms of abandoned houses, the zombies lurked, waiting for night.

CHAPTER 8

STOWAWAY

I kept low as I walked the long stretch of concrete by the bay to a ship docked by the pier. It looked like most of the cargo vessels were departing the Manila North Harbor Container Port. Men frantically readied ships to take to the sea. At the perimeter of the pier, the steel fence guarding the property held back a slew of zombies. Just barely. The monsters shook the fence, shrieked at seeing "food" they couldn't reach.

Some began climbing.

Taking advantage of the mad scramble, I dashed for a docked shipping vessel, approaching from the coast where there was no fence. The ramp was empty, and no one stood guard. I snuck down the ramp to the deck, then circled around to the cargo area. There were tons of container ports, yet few guards. I settled into a shadowed spot and listened for signs the zombies had crossed the fence.

Men shouted. The ramp was pulled in. Screams came from the dock. Water splashed: the sound of swimming. The ship captain ordered the men to take them in. "All engines go!" he cried. "Don't turn back! Those things are waiting for us!"

I snuck a peek. Men were being lifted from the bay with ropes and lifelines. On the pier, zombies chased staffers. Hunted them down. The zombies boarded docked shipping vessels, tearing into crewmembers' faces and necks. Armed guards tried fighting but pistols couldn't fend off the large numbers. Smoke permeated the dank air; there were dark, billowing clouds. Men screamed; bodies twitched violently as zombies feasted on them. Vessels unlucky enough to stay docked during the onslaught served up crewmembers like a buffet.

Three vessels survived the zombie outbreak and sailed in a tight pattern. I waited anxiously behind a container at the back of the holding area, hoping no one would find me.

But words from the captain had my heart racing: "Check for stow-aways. Zombies especially! Don't leave one on this ship, or it will kill us in our sleep!"

Would they throw me overboard if they found me?

"Make damn sure!" the captain shouted.

I sat shaking, waiting for the search party. Outrunning the crew was my only option. What other choice did I have?

I stayed alert in the dark where the containment units were stored below deck. Like the Tondo slums in daybreak, the steel units presented plenty of places to hide and wait. I watched for flashlights heading into my aisle, turned the corner to the left side, slipped behind another container and hid again.

The men flashed their lights this way and that, but I was one step ahead of them. Always light on my bare feet, I was as quiet as a mouse while I trotted between aisles fleeing one search party member after another. I could do this forever.

When I turned the next corner, a man with a flashlight forced me to my left again. I held my breath as my heart pounded. Another man flashed his light from the farthest end. I had unwittingly backed myself into a corner at the very last containment unit. I hesitated. Saw other lights head their way, both upfront and behind. They were systematically searching from each containment unit until the very last one on the corner was cleared.

No choice but to fight now. As soon as the guard turned the corner from upfront, I knocked him down and made a run for it. Radios crackled with static and loud voices as I fled the cargo area. I dashed toward the cabins below deck when a man knocked me down and pointed a gun at me.

"Well, well, what do we have here?" the captain said, his gun inches from my face. He crouched, gun now pressed firmly against my head. He examined my eyes then parted my lips to see my teeth. He frowned. "A stowaway? But not a zombie? Hmmm..."

"What now, sir?" one of the other guards said, catching his breath as the others raised their oars and iron bars as if to strike.

"No. Put down your weapons. He's not a zombie," the captain said with frustration. "Proceed with your search. Leave no stone unturned."

I stared at the captain, my mouth open, scared it was going to be the end of me.

"You, child," he said. "Come with me."

———— ◦ ————

Guards continued searching the deck, the cargo area, the cabins below deck, the engine bay, and the mess hall. I heard it all from the captain's quarters, where I sat at a table opposite the man, a window behind him giving me a view of the sea.

The captain studied me from across the table, stroking his mustache. His thick, wavy, black hair was tucked beneath his captain's hat. His windbreaker was now hung on a coat hook near the door, and his muscles strained against his navy-blue polo shirt.

His stare was sharp, and he very much reminded me of General Luna.

"Kapitan Ruiz," he finally said, introducing himself, lighting a cigarette as he watched me.

I was scared of him, but I managed to say my name. "Luzvimindo, po."

He raised his chin at me, those eyes examining me once more. "How did you get on board?" he asked, blowing smoke over his shoulder.

I rubbed my hands together, trying to stay calm. "While chaos was ensuing portside, I crossed the ramp to the ship."

He smiled...somewhat, but had yet to ask where I lived, where my family was. "What I meant to ask was, how did you survive the zombie outbreak?"

Tears streamed down my cheeks when I remembered Mama, Papa, Laleng, and Jason. Remembered Enrico and Bodjie turning on us. "I almost died many times."

Captain Ruiz eased back into his chair and turned to look out the window at the smoke spiraling from the bay. Tondo looked as though it was intentionally being burned for metals, like what scavengers did to plastics to obtain copper wire in the landfills. The zombies still rampaged through the streets. The smoke stretched as far as the eye could see: Navotas to Tondo to Intramuros to Pasay.

"My wife and son are dead, Luzvimindo," Captain Ruiz said without turning to face me. "A witness told me they were attacked during the outbreak. *Hindi na ako umuwi*. I didn't come home. I didn't want to see them changed into those things."

He faced me again, tears welling in his eyes, but he held them back—a hardened man. His lips spoke hatred: hatred for those things, hatred for the misery of never seeing his wife and child, hatred for what he believed to be cowardice on his part. "I will protect you as long as you're on board. We are applying for asylum in the United States. Once we get there, you're on your own, okay?"

I nodded and wiped away my tears, feeling a lot less scared.

He smiled, and a teardrop escaped his eye. "Have you eaten yet?" he asked. "Maybe you're hungry."

Captain Ruiz and I were in the mess hall, and he watched me wolf down fried chicken, *siomai*—I loved pork dumplings—and white rice. It was my first clean meal since losing Jason. The captain smiled like he was happy to see me eat. He spoke into his walkie-talkie occasionally, asking for updates from the search party.

The broken chatter from the radio turned into silence, and Captain Ruiz faced me once more. I bit into my chicken leg, then scooped up rice from my plate with my hand.

"You remind me a bit of my son, Luzvimindo," he said, glancing in all directions, still worried about the zombies. "He eats like that. Especially when I come home with good food."

I smiled and said, "Thank you, po, for the food." I chowed down like a hungry street cat. The plate was clean after ten minutes. Captain Ruiz motioned over to the chef to fill up my glass with some cold water.

"Captain!" someone said from his radio. "We found a body. He looks like he was eaten!"

Captain Ruiz's eyes sharpened. His fearsome demeanor returned instantly. "What area? How many are down? Ask for a head count of the search party!"

The voice didn't reply right away. When the radio crackled to life again, Captain Ruiz indicated that it was time for us to head back to his cabin.

"One down, Captain. Search party reports fifteen remaining men."

"We're undermanned as it is. We can't lose anyone else. Split into twos and proceed with your search. Over and out."

Captain Ruiz promptly replaced his seat. I rushed to wipe my hands and mouth with the table napkins. When we exited the mess hall into the hallway, he gestured for me to stay close. We climbed the stairs to the deck and entered his quarters.

"*Putang ina*!" Captain Ruiz exclaimed in his cabin. He lost his composure and slammed his hat onto the floor before picking it up and slapping it on the hanger. He took out a gun from the drawer in his desk. "Stay here, Luzvimindo. Hide. I'll lock the door. I have to see to the victim's body. We may have a zombie on board," he said before leaving in a mad rush. The doorknob shook, indicating it was locked from outside. I sat there shivering, wondering whether they would find the zombie stowaway.

———— • ————

Captain Ruiz returned to the cabin, bent forward, demoralized. I came out of hiding and approached him cautiously.

"We have a stowaway," he said grimly. "The body of the crewmember was barely whole." I waited for him to continue as he paced the room. "He was eaten."

Thunder clapped outside. The winds picked up and the skies grew darker. The waves tossed violently against the starboard side.

"We've given the man a proper burial at sea," he said further, ice in his throat. "My crew believe you are the zombie."

I shook my head. Surely, they didn't believe it.

"I told them you weren't. I was certain." He sighed. "They said if not you, then who?" There was a sliver of doubt in his eyes; they no longer glared like smoldering coals in the Tondo charcoal pits. "I told them I didn't know. That we had another stowaway, and to just keep searching."

He stared at me now, like he was making his mind up. He eased his shoulders, approached me, and put a hand through my hair. "I'm scared, and I don't want to admit it," he said. "So is my crew, Luzvimindo." He turned his gaze to the view of the open sea, white foam-capped waves tossing in the pitch-dark night. "The zombies are more active at night. This is the time they like to hunt."

<hr />

The first night proceeded without further problems. After a checkup in sickbay, we ate breakfast at the mess hall the next morning, and I sat next to Captain Ruiz, who chewed on toast and eggs while I ate a ham sandwich and drank orange juice.

The men spoke enthusiastically despite the zombie still loose. Perhaps we were reassured because we were numerous. I doubted whether the crewmembers weren't still nervous though.

For that brief time, any of the apprehension about me being on board the ship was gone. They told stories about loved ones before the zombie outbreak, about places they'd visited. Captain Ruiz asked his right-hand man, Lieutenant Galenza—a lean, narrow-faced man with a mustache and thinning hair—what his family's last excursion had been.

"Christmas, at La Union, Kap. I took my family: my wife, Ellen, my kids, Ricardo and Erica. First, we dropped by the beach. Then, we went down to my parents' place at Cabanatuan to eat for *noche buena*. After eating, the kids opened their gifts," Galenza said.

"I've met your family, Lieutenant," Captain Ruiz said. "I'm glad you enjoyed your trip with them. Wasn't the *longganisa* you bought from that town delicious? I remember that you even shared some of it with us on your return trip."

Galenza nodded. "I also bought *longganisa* from Lucban once. That was good too."

"What about Pampanga Tocino? I mean, the real thing. Not the supermarket product," Captain Ruiz asked everyone. "Don't tell me none of you have tasted the real thing?"

A sailor named Emil, a round-faced, chubby, dark man with messy hair, spoke up. "We've eaten them at a feast in San Fernando. They also served roasted catfish, roasted pampano, and *lengua estofado*—the ox tongue was so tender," he said. "I took my entire family, Kap. My wife, Juanita, and my two children, Rex and Defonso."

Captain Ruiz smiled at the man. "We can't find enough time to go on trips when we're on vacation. Chalk it up to the life of a seaman."

I ate, listening to the chatter and laughter filling the room. Enthusiastic descriptions of places and food were offered by everyone. When the talk mellowed, the walkie-talkie sounded off like a man was in a state of panic.

"Kap, we've found another corpse! You need to come see this right away!"

Captain Ruiz stood, and the rest of us followed. He suddenly turned to face me. "Keep close!" he said, then placed his index finger against his lips and turned to the others.

Everyone nodded.

We took the stairs from the mess hall to another set of stairs heading below deck to the engine bay. Then traipsed down a long series of dark corridors, networks of pipes lining the rails to the sides and on the ceiling, hot steam occasionally blowing from valves overhead.

When we reached the engine bay, two men were standing watch at the door. They told Captain Ruiz they had found the chief engineer dead on the floor in the corner of the engine bay, still holding his clipboard and pen—killed while making routine checks.

I kept close to the captain as he approached the corpse. There was the chief engineer, his face mauled and half-gone, his heart and liver extracted like trophies.

Captain Ruiz examined the mess of meters and pressure valves, the large console wet with the engineer's blood. The captain read engine performance meters and bar-graphs, a look of confusion dawning on his face. Should the ship run into trouble, fixing things would be difficult without the engineer.

"Why was he down here without anyone? I gave orders for everyone to go in twos! Nobody goes alone!" he cried out. The other men humbly stared. The captain's concerns were justified. They were undermanned, and they'd lost a vital member of the crew to an oversight.

"Hunt this thing down! I want all available resources!" Captain Ruiz said. The men dispersed. Lieutenant Galenza and I stayed with the captain. He was seething, pushing a hand through his hair while pacing the room. He finally refocused and gestured for us to follow. Galenza took the rear, making sure nothing would creep up from behind. Captain Ruiz, gun in hand, led us down the main corridor heading upstairs. He watched for signs of movement, through large pipes and valves and other rooms, telling Galenza there was too much ground to cover, too few search teams to comb through the entire ship and root out every possible hiding place. We headed to his quarters.

"Hide, Luzvimindo," Captain Ruiz said. "I'll return after helping the search."

<hr />

Captain Ruiz came back, wiping sweat off his forehead, and I came out of hiding from his closet, emerging from behind a wall of coats and suitcases, scared that the thing would finish off Captain Ruiz and his crew.

He looked relieved to see me, and I met him with some degree of optimism. He could tell.

Captain Ruiz shook his head. "This thing is tricky, Luzvimindo. It moves around and hides in the dark."

"Min," I replied. He looked puzzled. "Min," I repeated. "It's my nickname,"

"Okay, Min," he said, smiling this time. He sat and rubbed his aching feet. "It must drive you nuts to hide in there," he said. "What do you do to pass the time?"

I was nervous to tell him the truth, but I came out with it anyway. "I cry. A lot at first. I remember my family and friends."

He nodded, a sad expression coming over his face. He went to the bathroom to shower. I sat at the table and waited for him.

An hour later, we were back in the mess hall. The crewmembers ate in shifts, two at a time. Men were needed to watch the bridge, the decks, and the engine bay. There weren't enough men, so Captain Ruiz and I ate by ourselves.

Dinner was fried chicken, a *pandesal*, a bread I hadn't had in a long time, and sopas—standard macaroni soup. I ate quietly while Captain Ruiz stayed alert for both of us. The chef and his assistant came out to serve the food and drink, and they spoke with Captain Ruiz. Both were scared and wanted desperately to call for help from a foreign country.

Captain Ruiz addressed their concerns. "We're in the middle of World War Three with these things right now. America has tightened its borders. Most of Southeast Asia is under attack. We're not even cleared to dock at Guam or Hawaii, and Japan has closed its ports. We have been instructed to seek asylum at Los Angeles Port of Entry. It's the only way in." He nodded at the two men. "*Manalig ka*, Chef. Have faith," he said with fierce determination. "We'll make it!"

The chef and his assistant didn't nod or agree, they looked somber and defeated. The monster on board was picking us off one by one. These were zombies, weren't they? We all wondered how it knew what it was doing. How it was smart enough to hunt the way it was.

Several days passed without incident. Already, we had sailed a long distance from Manila. We were crossing the Pacific without problems, yet Captain Ruiz was still nervous. He was losing sleep, which I knew from sleeping on a mattress on the floor nearby. I had trouble sleeping as well. The nightmares kept me up. Fear pricked like needles at my senses, and when I did manage to fall asleep, I woke bathed in sweat. Only the exhaustion gave us all respite, providing us some much-needed rest for a couple hours. Always, we rose with heavy limbs. We showered briskly, ate our meals like men starved.

Captain Ruiz and the men decided to organize another search. Thirteen men, with Captain Ruiz joining Lieutenant Galenza and a sailor to split up and search the ship from top to bottom.

The hours that passed were nerve-wracking. Again, I hid in the closet and cried over memories that flickered like a rolodex of images in my mind. I remembered Mama and Papa smiling and mussing my hair after I got home from school; Papa congratulating me for finishing each grade level in the top ten of my batch by buying me some Sorbetes ice cream. I remembered Mama bringing us extra dishes from the canteen where she worked as part of her bonus for the holidays. We were full those nights, eating queso de bola and various entrees.

I remembered Laleng's smiling face, the other students laughing at us, calling us *mag-siyota*, although we were never dating. She would tell me about missing us once we graduated, and how she would work abroad as a nurse. I encouraged her to chase her dreams, telling her that she wouldn't miss Bodjie's *pang-aasar*, his teasing.

Images rose of Jason showing us some cool pictures from his smart-phone, letting us watch YouTube videos while we laughed and joked. He was humble and down-to-earth about his own dreams of working in automotive tuning, getting a car, souping it up, and racing with friends on the track on weekends away from work.

And Enrico being the first guy to contradict everyone in the *bark-ada*, the sarcastic one, pessimistic by nature. He would sneer whenever someone ended up wrong about something, saying he had been right all along, and all of us would burst out laughing in the end. Enrico always softened up when you needed him to be a friend, no longer sarcastic and biting, but reassuring and encouraging instead.

How I missed Bodjie's loud, raucous laughter, especially after teasing and taunting to get conversations started. He used to scour the landfills with me like a true childhood companion, never missing a day even though the others might skip. Bodjie was my *resbak,* my back-up, my wingman, and never let other boys push me around. I felt his loss more intensely that day. I was unsure why. Mama and Papa were watching over me from heaven, I knew that. Laleng and Jason too. However, Enrico and Bodjie were zombies, still trapped in their bodies. I wanted to take Captain Ruiz's gun and shoot them, free them from their undead prisons. I couldn't stand the thought that they were still feeding somewhere, still hurting other people.

Suddenly, Captain Ruiz entered and called out for me excitedly. "Min," he said. "Come out now! We found the zombie. It's dead!"

I couldn't believe it. "Is it really dead?"

"Come with me, Min. Do you want to see?"

I hesitated, remembering the scavenger-zombies of Tondo. I was scared, but managed to nod. "Yes."

Captain Ruiz led the way, and I raced to keep up, sometimes running into him because I was too busy glancing behind us.

The zombie was in a seldom-used closet in the holding area for rescue boats, twisted limbs making it resemble a desiccated mummy from an Egyptian tomb.

"There," Captain Ruiz said. "We found it this morning," he told me, pointing.

The crowd of sailors stood by silently, all watching and smiling.

I examined it for signs of life. It *looked* dead. It didn't move. Its eyes were open, yellow and cloudy. The teeth were shiny, yellow, and the gums black; a little black liquid trailed from the corner of its mouth. It was a female. She looked like a wraith, like a witch without the black hood and cape. She wore a torn t-shirt and shorts. Her remaining hair was gray and frizzy, like Spanish moss. Her dry, brittle skin looked like ground laminate. Her shriveled tissues contorted in an expression of pain, and her hands and feet had gnarly, disfigured fingers and toes.

"What is that fluid coming out of her mouth?" I asked Captain Ruiz.

"Must be blood," Captain Ruiz said. "Nothing to worry about."

The crewmembers and I were in the mess hall celebrating with Captain Ruiz. The chef and his assistant served some fresh catch from the sea: several crabs and mussels. Everyone broke off pincers and used small pairs of pliers to break the shells, scooping up fat and meat and greedily gorging on them.

Captain Ruiz had lost all the apprehension he carried over the past week. We were steadily crossing the Pacific, ready to make radio contact with Los Angeles Port of Entry, ready to face our new lives away from the horror on our native soil. Captain Ruiz led the men in prayer, so I, too, bowed my head reverently. We gave thanks for our meal, for the zombie's passing, and for our imminent rescue and escape from Armageddon. He even told the crewmembers that I would become a seaman once I came of age. I laughed along, of course. I was proud of Captain Ruiz. I would have been proud to serve as a crewmember now that I had let go of my dreams of becoming a doctor. I had a new family.

Captain Ruiz raised his glass to make a toast. "Let's remember this, boys!" he began. "To all of us, to our new lives as free Americans, for our family and friends who didn't make it."

We all raised our glasses. The crewmembers were having beer, I had a glass of orange juice. We clinked glasses, and Captain Ruiz turned to address me. "Min," he said to me proudly, like a father. "I'll adopt you when we reach the United States. I have no more family left. They're gone. So are yours. We have each other. We'll start over as a family."

Then he addressed everyone else. "We all have each other—"

An alarm sounded. The lights flickered. The chef came to the mess hall and quickly approached Captain Ruiz. "It's coming from sickbay," Chef said with a red face. "It must be Emil. He was bitten by that zombie in the cargo bay. This might not be over."

Captain Ruiz looked at the chef intently, unable to disguise his shock. He led the men out of the mess hall and down the hallways to sickbay to check on the patient.

I recalled my own observations of the zombie outbreak. If Seaman Emil were bitten, he would have likely turned into a zombie like the one we found.

When we arrived at sickbay, the door was open and smeared with blood. Inside, a grisly scene awaited us. The body of the ship's surgeon lay mangled, mauled, and eviscerated from the top of the examining table, blood pouring forth. Smatterings of guts clung to the walls, medical equipment, and instruments everywhere. Somewhere in the doctor's belly, in the middle, was a hollow opening for a liver, pancreas, and spleen. His bowels hung like sausage links from the table. His expression still held the excruciating pain of his death.

Captain Ruiz turned from the body and faced the crew. Some crewmembers threw up their celebratory lunches on the hallway floor. Lieutenant Galenza didn't. He stopped short of suppressing his nausea and waited for Captain Ruiz to give the order.

"This thing bit Seaman First Class Emil, and now Emil is a zombie. Take extra precaution to hunt Emil down before nightfall. We're almost at Los Angeles. We need to find him before he kills anyone else!"

I was back in Captain Ruiz's closet, anxiously awaiting the results of the search. Several hours must have passed before the door finally clicked open, and Captain Ruiz's voice offered me quick solace. It was evening, and he looked very tired.

He also looked sad. He wasn't wounded. He pulled his gun from its sachet and reloaded it at the dresser. Then he told me he was taking a shower. The door was locked, so he assumed we were safe.

"We lost more men today, Min. Good men," he said with a hint of surrender. "No. Emil's not dead yet. We're outmatched. We have only one gun and several paddles and iron bars as weapons. I lost four men today. They were bitten. They were going to turn into zombies, so I shot them."

I could only look on. He said one last thing before closing the door. "Galenza is dead too. He was my best man at my wedding."

I sat on the floor and waited. Then, an alert signal came on. Captain Ruiz rushed out of the bathroom, half-dressed. He grabbed his pistol and told me to hide. I went back inside the closet and listened for noises. There were all kinds of sounds coming from below deck, shoes banging on the steel staircase, thudding on walls, grunting, screaming, then gunshots.

For a while, all was quiet. When Captain Ruiz didn't return, I slipped from the closet and peeked outside the cabin window.

Nothing.

Suddenly, the doorknob rattled. I jumped, heart thumping, and raced back to the closet and barricaded my space with the suitcases, shivering with terror.

"Min, come out," Captain Ruiz said.

Fear kept me in, still hidden; I didn't know whether he had been bitten, whether he had morphed into a zombie even.

"Min, it is safe."

Captain Ruiz waited patiently for me to finally emerge, and when

I did, I found him with blood on his shirt, the gun held loosely in his hand. When he saw me, he dropped it on the floor. "They're all dead," he said. Then, he broke down, crying. "So is Emil though."

He dropped to the floor, sobbing. I stepped toward him, wanting to give him a hug, but he stopped me short. He tried to speak through tears. "I've radioed help for you. The American Coast Guard will come pick you up. I told them you haven't been bitten. You'll get on the lifeboat in the cargo bay, and they will locate you on the ocean. They have our coordinates. They will find you."

I burst into tears. I shook my head. "You're coming with me."

"I'll take you over to cargo bay, to the lifeboats," he said. "Once I release your boat, you will be on the ocean, waiting for rescue. Understand? We don't have much time."

I continued resisting Captain Ruiz's instructions, shaking my head vigorously and crying. But then, he suddenly turned around and revealed a sizeable wound on his upper back. It was discharging black ooze. Angry teeth marks left threads of skin loose along the jagged edges. Captain Ruiz's veins leading from the wound were growing visibly blue under the skin, like snake venom spreading rapidly from the point of infection.

Minutes later, Captain Ruiz strapped a lifejacket around my chest and waist and asked me to sit in the lifeboat. He looked at me closely one more time before he smiled and shed another tear. "I'll remember you, Luzvimindo," he began. "You are my other son. Don't forget me." He tugged at my lifejacket, making sure it was fitted perfectly. He held my shoulders and then abruptly let go. I felt light-headed, dizzy with fear and despair.

Tears rolled down my cheeks as I watched him turn around and head to a lever by the wall of the cargo area. I couldn't stop crying.

I couldn't believe what was happening. Mama, Papa, Laleng, Jason, everyone. Gone. Now Captain Ruiz was going to die too. I couldn't fathom it.

Then, before I could get out of my seat and run to Captain Ruiz like a son on the first day after school, he smiled. It was a big, warm smile. I tried to reach out for him, persuade him to come with me, but he pulled the lever down, and the lifeboat dropped into the ocean. I sat in the boat, peering high up at the cargo bay wanting to see Captain Ruiz, but the lifeboat just kept drifting away.

The ship's engine was still running, and it moved farther and farther away. I kept searching the deck, hoping to see Captain Ruiz just one last time.

A gunshot rang out.

CHAPTER 9

ASYLUM

I was stuck in a facility in Los Angeles for three days before I spoke to anyone else. Besides me, there were crewmembers from other vessels entering United States waters. I learned quickly how the Americans were responding to the global zombie pandemic—turning away the wounded, regardless of whether the crewmembers said they were bitten or not, leaving them on ships and offering only first aid equipment. They tested us for drugs. What drugs, exactly, I didn't know.

They didn't guarantee asylum either. Only said we could apply. I overheard someone say the Americans just wanted information from us; either that, or they were going to run tests on us. We would be deported anyway.

What information the U.S. wanted, I didn't know exactly. I guessed it was about the zombie pandemic. What the situation was like in our respective countries, what we did to survive, what we'd seen.

In the meantime, they gave us food, drink, and clothing.

I was told that the United States was able to quarantine against an outbreak on their shores. There were a few exceptions—cases when police and military had to contain threats. More crewmembers reasoned that the Americans orchestrated the entire pandemic to eliminate every other major nuclear power in the world. I didn't want to believe it. America didn't need to drive both allies and enemies to extinction if it wanted to upset the balance of power. A pandemic like this would have reached U.S. shores after some time. I was too young to know, but it seemed ludicrous to think the Americans would hatch a biological weapon capable of destroying more than half the population (including their own). It would send their own economy into ruin; if not right away, eventually. The offending party had to be a nation with aspirations of usurping America's place in the hierarchy, a genocidal regime like the Nazis. I refused to believe that the Americans could have been responsible. I needed to know I could be safe somewhere. Where else would I go now?

I was just trying to get out alive without being deported. I was finally interviewed after I completed the observation process. I guess they wanted to see if I would morph into a zombie before letting me out of my cell.

"Good day, Mr. Arnaiz. How are you, young man?" a soldier in a combat uniform asked. Perhaps he was an army officer.

"I'm fine, sir. Thank you for asking," I answered politely.

The gentleman appeared to be impressed with my decorum, my engaging smile, and my fluency. I liked that he was pleased.

"How old are you?" he asked.

"I'm twelve years old, sir." I sat at attention in my chair, not leaning against the table with my arms or elbows as if I was lazy. I was in the presence of the military, so I tried to behave appropriately.

"Where are your parents, if I may ask? And what's your first name?"

He noticed my expression change, and sobered up to the realization that things were truly brutal where I'd been.

"I'm Luzvimindo, sir. My nickname is Min. My parents are dead, sir."

"Was the ship captain your father?"

I didn't cry while he was questioning me. I was holding up. "Captain Ruiz?" I said. "He's not. He's like a dad though. I've only known him for a short time, but he's a very good man. He saved my life."

The man in uniform swallowed hard. "I'm sorry to hear it. Captain Ruiz's ship was stopped before proceeding further into U.S. waters. It was boarded. I'm very sorry to tell you that he was found dead, along with the other men on the ship."

I nodded my understanding.

"What happened back in Manila? And what part of Manila are you from?"

"I'm from Tondo. Barangay Happyland in Tondo. A very poor area, sir."

I paused. He waited for me. Someone came to our room and placed a glass of water on the table. Then the gentleman smiled to let me know to continue. I was only repeating what I told customs officials the day they welcomed me to their shores.

"The drug addicts, sir. They began morphing into zombies. When these zombies bit people, those people turned into zombies too. Sometimes the zombies attacked people and didn't transform them. They ate them, especially when the victims couldn't get away. They ate their livers, innards, choice meats. Soon, the whole of Tondo was overrun with these things and the buildings were on fire. People were screaming. Police couldn't fight them. You couldn't tell which ones were which during the mad scramble."

The man nodded to someone behind the mirror. Then, the gentleman slowly leaned forward and jostled in his seat, finding the right words to say to me as he rolled his eyes and scanned the room for a light to switch on.

"It's happening all around the world, Min. We're one of the few countries left that has yet to see an outbreak. We'll place you in a temporary residence while you get approved for a visa and get back with you if we have any questions. It's important that when you are transported to your new residence you refrain from going outside, loitering in the streets, and avoid any use of illegal drugs. Is that understood?"

I nodded. I had a million questions in my head but didn't have the courage to ask them.

"You'll have a probation officer that will explain more details. You'll be given a supply of food and transported to Rochester, New York, where you will reside until you are approved for lawful residence in the United States of America," he said formally, like he had memorized it.

My eyes welled. I missed my parents, my friends, Captain Ruiz and the crew. I was alone here. America was a big country. Like a desert island the size of a continent. I wondered whether there was any place in Manila or the entire Philippines that made it out safe from the chaos.

"Welcome to America," the gentleman in uniform announced gladly. He looked sad to see me alone, but was pleased to know I would survive here. He shook my hand lightly and then left. I remained in my cell until late that night when the guards woke me up to transport me cross-country to Upstate New York.

They learned that I had a fever before I made the trip to Rochester. They took my temperature right before departure. I also began coughing and going to the boy's room often. The nursing techs took swab tests. I was positive for coronavirus. I hadn't used a mask in more than a week and was quarantined in a facility with frequent foot traffic. I guessed my luck had run out in the port of Los Angeles. My time in Tondo, Manila, was shockingly COVID-free despite scavenging for money. It didn't matter where I'd picked up the virus, I was lucky to be stable.

The staff fitted me with an N95 mask, and two military officers got in a black SUV with me. We got out at an airport where we hopped on

100

a military plane. They let me lie on a stretcher and gave me antibiotics while on the flight.

When we landed at an airstrip in Fort Lee, New Jersey, we got in a vehicle and headed for Rochester. The roads were smooth. The views were open and expansive, and the trees and landscaping at the roadside looked meticulously cared for. I loved how America looked, what with the new cars and wide roads, beautiful buildings and charming lawns, but I missed everyone I knew. I was scared I wouldn't survive here.

I was twelve.

The officer in the seat next to me said I would make it. My COVID infection wasn't the serious kind. "You're lucky. With everything else you've been through, that COVID's still not strong enough to fight a zombie-killer," he said, chuckling afterward. The driver of the vehicle laughed along. They were trying to raise my spirits, but I felt too sick to join in or disapprove. He smiled and let me rest.

We reached a fenced-off estate in the woods guarded by a military checkpoint. The driver spoke to the guards, and we were promptly allowed inside. It was a long drive before we reached the first batch of houses. The place was like a camp. It looked deserted.

When we arrived at one of the buildings, some of the yards had broken furniture like old bedsprings, old tables, and chairs with missing legs. There was garbage littering some of the lawns, even right outside the trash bins. There were old toys beside doorsteps, an old doll with a half-twisted-off head, a broken toy car for a toddler to pedal. The place was quiet though. No neighbors.

It was a ghost town.

The military officers escorted me out of the vehicle and showed me to the door of the unit. I was so sick, I just wanted to lie down. Inside, it smelled moldy and stuffy, but still better than Tondo by any stretch. The place was small by American standards, but it all felt like I was given a pass out of a hard life. There was an upstairs bedroom and bathroom.

Downstairs, there was an eat-in area, kitchen, living room, and foyer. It was furnished.

"Pretty basic for a single, unwed asylum seeker, but you'll get used to it," the previous gentleman seated next to me during the ride said. "We're not leaving you hanging, okay? We're deploying a nursing aide to make routine checks on residents every twelve hours."

The other officer spoke up. "The doctors said you would recover without the need for in-patient hospitalization. The hospitals are on high alert right now, considering the situation all over the world. You've probably seen what could happen in a hospital during this pandemic, haven't you?"

I nodded, clutching the blanket around my shoulders tighter. The two men showed me upstairs. There were clothes ready for me in the closet. They looked a little big.

"These look like American-sized juniors clothing," the first guy said, spreading out a sweater to have a look before folding it back up. The other officer checked the bathroom for running water. He tugged at the light switch and the bulb came on. He opened the faucets and closed them. The first guy checked the baseboard heating and turned the nightlamp on. Satisfied with their inspection, the two men faced me again.

The first guy spoke. "You let us know if you need anything, champ, okay? You can call that number by the phone downstairs."

I took my shoes off and lay in bed. I tucked my tired bones in, and the friendly officer helped. He smiled like a visiting uncle.

The bed was soft, and the sheets were clean. It was like Manila hotel compared to Barangay Happyland's Tondominiums—our shanties constructed from industrial garbage.

Once the two men left, I lay in bed and stared at the ceiling, listening for noises—neighbors possibly turning into zombies, groaning in the wee hours, starved for food. Despite being assured that America was safe, I was extremely frightened.

———— • ————

The next morning, I was told to quarantine for a week. In the meantime, they had stocked my pantry with food. There was canned meat and canned fruit. I took a box from the shelf and read the label. *What is Hamburger Helper?* I opened a fruit cup and a can of sardines and ate. I was coughing a little. I bit my lip, and took some water from the sink out of a water filter attached to the faucet. The water tasted clean, so I was comforted. Tondo was nothing like this.

I was at the dining table eating my food when the front door opened. It was the nursing tech, wearing scrubs and a mask, carrying a black leather doctor's bag. Her hair was braided, and dyed red and brown; her hazel eyes bright against her black skin.

"Good morning," she said cheerfully, and set her bag on the table. She took my temperature, which was still high, and gave me some pills. "Antibiotics," she said, sounding just like a mom.

I couldn't tell whether she smiled at me underneath her mask, but she didn't seem like a typical government worker, just doing her job and hurrying to leave. Instead, she genuinely wanted to make sure I was well.

"It may be some time till the government arrives at a decision," she said. "So please take care of yourself. I left a bottle of vitamins in the pantry and some medicine on your dresser. Please follow the instructions," she said. "Do you have any questions so far?"

I had many. I asked the most obvious one. "Do I get to live here? I like this place."

Despite her mask, I could tell she looked sorry for me. "I'm not your probation officer, so I don't know the answer to that," she said. "I'm glad you're comfortable though." She listened to my breathing with a stethoscope. Then, she took a flashlight and looked into my nose and throat area, and continued to ask questions. "More diarrhea? Fatigue?"

I nodded. "Both."

She placed her things in her bag then did a swab test. Next, she placed the swab in a biohazard bag before she put that away too. "It will take a week for things to clear up. Maybe two weeks. We'll test you again," she said.

I nodded and lay down on the couch, telling her I felt woozy. It occurred to me to ask her something though. "Are there zombies coming out of nowhere here too?"

She studied me carefully, maybe concerned I'd been through some really intense trauma, which was true. "You're safe here," she said. "For now. Let's just hope."

I had been at my new home four days, sitting on the couch, watching TV. Besides that, I was also camping out in my bedroom with a blanket raised from the four corners of the bed. I was extremely lonely, homesick, and bored. I was trying to enjoy the better amenities: an American apartment was still better than any third-world slum. It's just that my parents couldn't enjoy it with me, and neither could my friends see it. I knew nobody. I sailed alone around my room like a kid playing make-believe. Today was my birthday. I'd just turned thirteen, and what a lucky number it truly was.

Still, I was alive and safe in a foreign country. The news showed scenes from across the world: India, Guatemala, Haiti, Ghana, Zaire, the Philippines. In each nation, the military fought off the zombie riots with diminishing resources. Cities burned. Survivors flocked into sanctuaries—they started out as tents in the mountains. Afterward, governments began constructing walls to seal off the communities.

The zombies flocked to any corner of the nation where human

blood could be found. The best place to build sanctuaries was in the mountains. The terrain was difficult to traverse by foot. The military transported people and supplies to and from the sanctuary via chopper. The sanctuaries were going to look like medieval castles.

The new world order had commenced.

Low-lying areas were abandoned. Cities became ghost towns. Governments predicted that once the zombies died out—they did, for some unexplained reason—then the towns would be safe again, assuming no one else was bitten. The zombies had a shelf-life, but they weren't certain how long. I remembered the zombie aboard Captain Ruiz's ship and agreed with those findings. A zombie would have to eat blood continuously to survive. It starved like any other human.

After four days passed and with only my nursing aide for occasional company (albeit very briefly), my probation officer came. He was a man with shoulder-length hair and a lazy-fitting suit. He said hello like some people said howdy.

"Is it Mindo or Min?" he asked very politely. He sounded friendly. His mask was on, but the lines on his face made it obvious he was grinning.

"It's Min," I answered. "I'm still sick." He was looking around, inspecting the dining area and kitchen. Without acknowledging my answer, he went upstairs for a while, probably inspecting the bedroom and bathroom as well.

"Well, Min, you've kept the place tidy. Listen, we have a hearing to attend as soon as you're well. They'll test you in a few days and we'll know then." He kept a tight expression, like he had just shared bad news.

I had a weird feeling I was going to be deported back to my country—now a warzone.

My nursing aide returned two days later. I'd gotten the urge to ask her name.

"Lakisha," she said warmly. "Pleased to meet you, Luzvimindo." I finally recognized her smile underneath her mask.

"My nickname is Min. Pleased to meet you, ma'am," I answered, still deferring to the designation of *ma'am* instead of her first name.

"Min, you're quite a nice young man," she said. "Tomorrow is your next swab test. I've just taken your first one. Two negative tests mean you're free to go to your hearing."

"I hope I get to stay."

"You don't sound so happy," she said, grimacing a little, wondering what was wrong.

"I don't know anybody," I replied. "Everyone I know back home is dead though. What do I have to go back to?"

She stared at me for long seconds, her expression kind of sad, but she didn't say she understood. "You must have been through hell. I wouldn't know what to do but stay here and get the hang of it. You can start over. I know it seems hard, but…" She put away my swab test and prepared to leave for the day. "Tomorrow, I do the next swab test, and then we'll know if you can attend your hearing. I'm crossing my fingers for you."

I crossed my fingers and tried to smile for her. She gave me a bigger smile than last time.

Once Lakisha left, I sat on the couch and turned on the news. Boy, did I get it!

The headline: *Asylum Seekers from Affected Countries Now Being Deported Due to Nationwide Panic!*

I learned that the hearing was a formality. Everybody was being turned away. Riots were erupting across America as people protested through the streets. The protesters had signs that read: *No Zombies On Our Doorsteps!* America didn't want us.

I looked around my living room and kitchen one more time.

It was time to plan my escape.

━━━━━◆━━━━━

I spent the night tossing and turning, nightmares of junkies transforming into bloodthirsty zombies hunting me throughout the streets of Tondo. In the dream, I was the last remaining survivor in the Philippines, and every day I had to hunt for food and supplies while dodging these new apex predators.

I stayed up from 3 a.m. onward. I didn't have coffee. I turned the TV on and tried to sleep on the sofa. By the time Lakisha came to do the last swab test at 8 a.m., I had napped for only a couple hours.

"You don't look good, Min. You'll need every ounce of strength you have. Here, take this," she said, handing me a pill. I hesitated but took it. I half-expected to drop dead after losing my trust in Americans. However, I perked up after some time.

Meanwhile, Lakisha was preparing her swab kit. "Raise your head toward me," she said, then inserted the cotton bud into my nostrils. She did another swab, and dropped the now-packaged samples into her bag and zipped it up. Then, she put it away and looked at me.

"I saw the news on TV," I said to her, probably looking like I was fleeced for marbles.

She looked as though something had knocked the wind from her sails when she shrugged, defeated. "Listen to the judge, Min, and hear what he has to say. You just never know. You're just a boy. I mean, unlike the others." She looked away with guilt and pain written on her face. I could tell she wanted to cry.

Me staring at her only made her feel worse. "I have a feeling I'll be sent back. They're building sanctuaries in the mountains there. Is that where I'll go?"

She couldn't look me in the eye, but I could tell she was trying to suppress her tears. "You just never know," she said. Then she did look.

Sadness broke like a river, and tears streamed down her eyes. She gathered her things and set them aside.

She hesitated, and I didn't know why. Then she hugged me. I realized she wasn't allowed to do that. I needed two negative swab tests to be cleared of contact, but she did it anyway.

When she walked out, I was resigned to being on the move again. I watched the news from across the world show scenes of fires burning, bombings, and shootings. Overseas, the military kept the zombies from climbing mountain roads. Checkpoints were poised at the foothills, missiles and large guns were aimed at all approaching trails. Helicopters provided safe transport. Fighter jets bombed zombie-infested areas. Villamor Air Base in the Philippines was one of the last military strongholds there. Camp Crame and Camp Aguinaldo were both evacuated due to both camps' locations in the heart of Manila, where the zombie outbreak was also raging.

While the walls of the sanctuaries were not yet completed, they were vulnerable to attack. These were the last bastions of society for such countries on the brink of destruction. Mountain ranges like the Cordilleras in the Philippines, where rebel factions often camped, were now hotbeds for these new civilizations. These mountains were so remote, they once offered refuge to Indigenous people who wanted to escape colonization from foreign invaders. Now, they were every surviving Filipino's only hope.

By the time the probation officer came with news, I had showered, eaten lunch, and was watching anime in the living room.

He walked through the door and waved. "Hello, Min. You're cleared," he said. "Are you ready to make the trip to the judge's chambers?"

I nodded, put on a flannel coat over my white t-shirt and black pants. Then, I laced my New Balance sneakers. "Ready," I said.

I smiled, and he returned the favor.

We walked outside and took a big breath. I had yet to see a family or any other person on the entire premises. It was still quiet, like an abandoned carnival, just things lying around. The two of us walked to his car, a Ford Fusion sedan, and got in.

After strapping on my seatbelt, I smiled at the officer.

He was wearing sunglasses. "Nice day, ain't it?" he asked.

I nodded again, and we drove out of the compound.

Houses and trees blurred along the road, making me wish I didn't have to return home. I didn't want another rollercoaster like my last days in Tondo.

We drove down the freeway at a relatively slow speed. Cars and trucks hurtled by. The officer asked me if I wanted the windows down. "Cool day today. Want to feel the breeze?" he asked.

I was glad he was laid back. "Sure," I said, like an American teenager. He rolled down my window with the touch of a button, and cool wind rushed though my hair. It felt like Baguio or Tagaytay in the Philippines, towns with cooler climate because they were way above sea level.

We eventually arrived at the Rochester town hall. Not New York City. We were just a short drive from my temporary residence.

It was a short walk up the steps to the courthouse, and the officer opened the door for me and followed me inside. We took our seats in the lobby and waited.

The officer was quiet. I tapped my shoes and patted my hands on my lap.

"Want something from the vendo?" the officer finally asked.

He must have realized I didn't know what a vendo was, and gestured toward the vending machine. It was the sweets that captured my attention and not the crackers. He watched me, his eyes crinkling with a smile behind his mask. He could tell I wanted a candy bar, a Snickers.

"You sure you don't want the crackers? It's got peanut butter," he said, teasing. "It'll give you some energy."

I looked at him and then at the vendo, and pointed at the Snickers.

"Good choice," he said. "I'll get you one."

I nodded.

He slotted two one-dollar bills in, and the Snickers bar tumbled to the bottom of the machine. He patted me on the shoulder when he handed it over. I peeled the wrapper and ate.

A short while later, the receptionist called us. The officer led me down the hallway to where two double doors waited. He knocked on the door and opened it, leading me inside a nicely appointed room with plenty of wooden furnishings. Seated across the desk was an older man in a judge's robe. I thought we were headed to a courtroom like I'd seen on TV.

"Please," the judge said. "Have a seat."

I sat and smiled at him. The officer whispered to me, "Refer to him as Your Honor, okay?"

Again, I nodded.

The judge smiled. "Well, young man. You've come so far to make it to our shores. How was your stay?"

I smiled. "Good," I said. "...Your Honor."

He smiled widely, seemingly pleased with my demeanor. He studied me closely, and I did the same of him. He had thinning white hair and pink skin, and kind of reminded me of Pope John Paul II, so I was relieved. Maybe he was going to be nice enough to let me stay, despite the news saying that asylum seekers from pandemic-affected countries would be rejected. I was hopeful. I was just a kid, like Lakisha had said. Listen to him, she had told me.

"Luzvimindo, I'm afraid I have some bad news for you," the judgesaid.

The rest was a blur. Me crying in the judge's quarters, pleading for him to let me stay. The officer calming me down. Me telling him about Mama and Papa, how my friends were dead, how everyone was. The judge spoke when I finally settled down, telling me the U.S. military would drop me off at Villamor Air Base with other detainees. They would take us to a sanctuary up the mountains. We could be with other Filipinos, start a new life there. He apologized repeatedly.

Later, the officer accompanied me out of the courthouse and back to the car. He explained the next steps on the way back. Two officers would fetch me at the residence and take me to the military base. Then they would fly me to the Philippines. I wasn't allowed outside my residence or outside the compound at any time. There were military men patrolling the perimeter of the residence as well as the compound. The probation officer apologized too, like the judge. I wiped my tears away and watched the road through foggy eyes.

I asked the officer to stop at a gasoline station so I could pee. He said yes. He pulled to the side and lit a cigarette. I got out and entered the convenience store to go to the restroom. Then I beelined to a truck parked some distance from the front. I hid behind one truck and the next one until I found a camper attached to an SUV at the front of the line. I tried the door of the camper and it was unlocked, so I got in. Right away, the SUV's engine came to life, and I was on the freeway in a matter of seconds.

I had made my daring escape.

When the vehicle stopped next, I was in New York City, at another gasoline station downtown. I got out while the driver was filling up, and I walked around, scared. Skyscrapers towered overhead, and stores and shops were filled with trendily dressed people.

I didn't know where to go and hide, so I headed down a staircase toward a subway station. When I found the blurring trains passing at high speed, rows of benches empty, derelicts seated against the wall, panhandling, I looked this way and that for an abandoned tunnel, somewhere safe from the cops. I found this guy hanging out nearby, waiting for a train. He was African American, wearing a sports jacket with a team logo over a pair of tight sweatpants. He said hi, and I reciprocated. He introduced himself. "My name's Mac. You don't know me, okay?" He smiled like he knew me well. Like he was friendly.

"Got some place to go? I can set you up," he said. "You must be new to below. You know, underground? I've never seen you around these parts. I'm an ambassador here."

I told him I was in-deep. He asked me to follow him.

So, as it turned out, Mac was a dealer. And that night he took me to the sewers. "Ain't pretty," he said. "And it doesn't smell good either. But at least you won't find cops here. That makes it prime real estate for people in your situation."

He took me to a spot in the sewers and briefly left me. The smell reminded me of Happyland and its open sewage. Here, in the sewers in America, you had more privacy. But it was haunting, dark, and claustrophobic being underground. There were better places to go, like the woods…but what did I know? I was newly deported and couldn't risk getting found by park rangers.

When Mac came back, he had a sleeping bag, a kerosene lamp, and a change of clothes. "Goodwill," he said with a grin. "I don't shop at the Salvation Army."

I smiled, thinking that I'd figure it out at some point. But then he took out a little plastic bag with powder in it and held it up to the light like a paper bill. "Induction," he said to me. "More like an indoctrination." He laughed like he didn't know what he was saying.

I knew what he was doing though. I was scared to say no. There was all this pressure mounting inside of me. I needed a place to stay. I needed to make friends, contacts.

He cut the white powder with a blade, then mixed it with a liquid base from another stopper, like he was mixing juice from concentrate, just in tiny amounts. He placed the liquid in a syringe.

I recalled my promise to my parents, my statement to Bodjie about doing drugs, my conversation with Doctor Amorsolo about kids who quit too young.

And none of it seemed to matter anymore when I pictured them turning into zombies. I wanted to forget, to deny, even though I said I wouldn't ever feel that way.

"Here," Mac said, handing over the syringe. "Take this, and you'll live."

PART 2

THE SECOND WAVE: WORLD DEMISE

CHAPTER 10

MY NEW HOME
NEW YORK CITY, 2027

It was seven years to the day since I first took heroin in the underground tunnels, and the world was on the cusp of dying. For years, I'd roamed these city streets, searching for my soul. I didn't see light when I saw lit streetlamps. I didn't see kind faces when I passed them on broken side streets. I didn't see compassion in the eyes of a generous person flipping a coin into my pan.

Strip-club signs shimmered with bright neon lights. Rundown bars were makeshift dives. Broken-down cars were suitable for maybe a night or two. In the city that never slept, *Wall Street Journal* readers read the headlines: *RIP New York City 2027*. The garbage bins were home to maggots, nests of cockroaches, and a milieu of unhappy faces.

I had a backpack full of clothes to wear regardless of season, one pair of shoes to comfort my weary soles. I didn't eat rancid meat, but I have tasted a sandwich or two from the bin outside the deli. The soup kitchen gave me free meals on occasion—no food stamps for groceries for me. I got cotton candy for dessert in garbage bins in Coney Island too.

Impoverished at the ripe old age of nineteen, I roamed the city and scoured for what I could sell: old lampshades and empty bottles and cans and even, on occasion, letters with personally identifiable information to use for identity theft.

I was a thief. But then again, who wasn't? Still, I refused to join small gangs of thieves desperate to steal any easy cash and drugs, even resorting to violence and murder. I ate at soup kitchens, frequently looted abandoned warehouses and shelters for cash and gadgets. I dashed through traffic-laden streets and climbed fences like a pro, dodging angry residents and police.

They might say, get a job. I asked them where? They might say, find a means to make a living. I asked them how? I was an illegal immigrant living in a time of economic crisis. The alternative was choosing to return to the Philippines, living in sanctuaries in the mountains under threat of zombie invasion.

All I had at the end of the day was enough to get by for another night in the subways: an ounce of heroin, a bottle of alcohol for my nightcap.

In the disconsolate winter, where many a vagabond on borrowed time had died due to the savage climate, I had survived years of jaundice, intestinal flu, and coronavirus. I compared hospital wards to hotel rooms, where I got free lodging above ground and free food fresh out of the oven. It all ended sooner or later. Before I knew it, I was back on the streets, eating buffet throwaways and old deli meat or canned soup served in Styrofoam bowls on lunch trays.

It always started at the place where it all began: a tunnel close to a strip mall in a bad part of Brooklyn, where the paved parking lots were broken, and weeds shot out of the cracks.

And it always ended back there—with the same silver spoon and kerosene lamp, the same knife and tourniquet, the same jelly jar I'd used for alcohol the past several years.

I'd been searching for my soul…

And wondering just how I'd lost it.

New York, post-Second Great Depression, had transformed into the slums of Tondo, post-new millennia. The worst slums in New York weren't simply tucked away from tourist spots any longer. They were everywhere. The poor gathered in large numbers.

Countries like the Philippines had ceased to be warzones, what with the largest groups of zombies supposedly dying out. The country was starting again, struggling with famine, sanctuaries in the mountains offering the safest dwellings for Filipino communities, but also far from fresh water sources. People didn't want to leave the highlands, fearing surviving zombies in the low-lying areas and cities. Those cities were ghost towns, charred buildings and ruins offering a reminiscence into the pandemonium that erupted years ago when the pandemic struck at full force.

I knew better than to resign myself to live in a city of decaying dreams, but New York was home now. I didn't actually have another place to go. The wealthier citizens erected gated, walled-off communities consisting of large acres of land in hillsides and mountainous regions across the country, similar to those sanctuaries in warzone-affected countries. They were also protected by the military.

For someone like me, the underground was still home. Yes, in modern-day New York City, drugs and alcohol were easy, cheap, and afforded a way out of a difficult life. The economic collapse meant food was scarce, prices were sky high, and staff jobs couldn't settle bills. Hourly wages were better suited for moldy cereal boxes, canned tuna, and a fix. I lay my bones to rest in a sleeping bag in the dark, used an old kerosene lamp for light, had books piled on top of one another, some on the very bottom sitting in the flowing sewage. The New York City skyline was a shroud beneath the funereal moon; home, for most, was a bed in an abandoned warehouse or apartment stacked with other beds.

Below was the best home for a child; it was easily safer than the streets. Once, when this was true and children were safer below than anywhere else, I met a single parent named Melanie who lived down here too. She was in her twenties and looked spry when in athletic clothing. She gushed after the time I gave her a candy bar.

"You're a lifesaver. What's your name?"

"Mindo," I said. "It's nice to meet you."

"Pleased to meet you too, Mindo. What a place to be making an acquaintance."

"The world is ending," I said. "We're all struggling to stay alive."

"I want my baby to survive. If not me."

I smiled, albeit sadly.

Within the sewers, her baby had a box with a pillow for a bed. Melanie stored their lives in a backpack she used when moving to different locations.

"Do you want to hold her?"

I said yes and gathered her baby from the box.

"Her name is Jenny," Melanie said, smiling.

I smiled down at the baby in my arms, giggled at Jenny, then returned her to her mom.

Melanie held Jenny close, then ate the Snickers bar as Jenny breastfed.

"I really appreciate you doing that for me, Mindo. I haven't eaten since yesterday."

I smiled again, and returned to Melanie's spot the next day to give her bread from the soup kitchen. We soon became friends.

———————— ◆ ————————

Underground was a cold, damp, dark paradise for rats and feral animals, both young and elderly vagrants who couldn't survive above ground. Most vagrants below lived in the abandoned subway tunnels close to Port Authority and Grand Central. Others like me, who were desperate to get away from crowds, lived a ways off, close to drainage systems leading into the bay—the tunnels still being accessible to desperate thugs. The subways stopped being safe years ago when the economic collapse drove more homeless people below. Police didn't patrol the stations. If a crime was committed, it wasn't investigated. Mac did a good job tutoring me about living below. "Make certain to dress like a hobo, don't make eye contact with anyone, and most of all, never wander out without a weapon," he said.

Spare change and drugs were a vagrant's most valuable commodities below. We made our way above ground to seek food, bringing shopping bags full of cheap bread and snacks down to the tunnels. So many young people relied on theft. Stealing was the most successful means of securing goods, including panhandling, scavenging, and bartering. Mac had a different opinion. "Stealing only gets you so much. Dealing fattens your pocket."

Nobody wanted to remember New York City in its heyday before the Second Great Depression hit the country, and global stock markets collapsed. World powers fell. Everyone fended for themselves. Unemployment numbers skyrocketed in many countries with vast populations, creating the threat of world war due to insurgency and famine. Tens of millions were dying from hunger: India, Africa, South America, Southeast Asia. Climate change altered the supply of livestock and produce, causing droughts or storm surges, even brutal winters or hot summers where both livestock and vegetation would die in massive numbers.

We were forced to watch it all happen: first on TV, when dictators altered the destinies of nations while isolationism quickly drove stocks to plummet. Then came the worsening effects of global warming: frequent category-five hurricanes, category-four tornadoes, waterways drying up, causing irrigation to suffer. Then we watched as people were evicted and foreclosures rose to alarming levels as unemployment surged. Once the streets were littered with vagrants, shelters were filled, and police couldn't stop the squatting and looting. With beautiful Central Park and the cobblestone walkways being the stuff of movies, New York City began to look like the slums again.

Mac set the scene for me in detail. "Thieves have proliferated in every district, in every borough and locale. Harlem has become a harem again. The Bronx is filled with tents and campsites. Long Island's affluent communities have retreated upstate, and their large studio lofts and bayside mansions are now occupied by well-off criminals and slumlords...like me," he said, smiling.

He went further. "Manhattan's yielded to urban decay; large flats and apartments facing Central Park have hit the dead housing market as wealthier entities and families have moved north where it's safer. Radio City Music Hall, Carnegie Hall, and Broadway have all become make-shift shelters, much like many apartment buildings by the bay. The theater seats are occupied by displaced residents. Police can't stop squatting even in Central Park; you'll find large groups of tents surrounding open campfires among the trees."

Acid rain in the year 2027, with the depleted ozone layer, forced vagrants like me below, instead of living in feeble cardboard boxes. The pre-dystopian age of New York City looked every bit as bad as New York City during the initial Great Depression. Enter the Second Great Depression, dubbed the Great Purgation—an age when civilization was close to complete collapse, and hordes of people were forced to find ways to survive.

It was dark and cold below, with the reinforced concrete walls locking in the winter chill. Aboveground, soup kitchens provided food and water away from the competition of large sewer rats numbering in the millions. Thieves and illegals like myself made a bed below ground because it was safer; the police didn't bother chasing even the most wanted criminals down to the abandoned tunnels and sewers. The safety net came at a price. You chose to survive, only to live like an animal.

When I wasn't high on heroin, meth, or cocaine, I read books in the sewers. As a scholarly child in Tondo, Manila—a lifetime ago—I also focused on reading. After years of knowing true horror, daily reality grotesquely twisted beyond the means to cope, I sought ways to divert my attention. Whenever the syringe or the bottle of painkillers was empty, whenever the alcohol ran dry, I read horror fiction with renewed eyes. Books by Richard Matheson and Brian Keene titillated my dulling imagination back to life. I fantasized being a hero in this alternate reality, fleeing the inauspicious circumstances of the real world.

I visited a used bookstore in Manhattan that had escaped looting. No one stole books. The storeowner was a genteel old man in a cardigan and glasses. Every day, it was a different color cardigan and trousers.

"Hello, Mr. Dunlap," I called out from the entrance. He'd smile and let me in. The door had an electronic lock and alarm. After all, even a bookstore had some spare change in the register.

"Hello, Luzvimindo." He called me by my first name, not nickname. I had elaborated on the origin of the name once when we got to talking, and he'd said that the historical reference made it way more interesting than most names.

He knew I was good business. Besides food, all I bought were drugs, booze, and books. He knew I was addicted to all of the above, but he trusted me because he said I was smart and always paid for any books I wanted.

"I think I may have an anatomy textbook with illustrations, like you wanted. This thing is huge, Luzvimindo. Do you think you can carry it below to the tunnels with you?"

"It might slow me down, Mr. Dunlap. Not to worry though. I don't suppose they'll take an interest in a medical book."

"No, I suppose not," he said, and handed me the book. "Pretty fine edition. No dog-eared pages," he said. "Just two dollars for that one. I purchased it for a buck. You're a regular customer."

I gave him the money, and we smiled at each other. "Thank you, Mr. Dunlap. I'll be back."

He looked reticent to let me go right away. "Uh, Luzvimindo?" he started, seemingly unsure whether to continue.

"Yes?"

"Get clean, will you?" he said. "There's hope for us all."

I smiled and saluted at him. He responded similarly.

When I left the bookstore, I trotted to the nearest subway tunnel and kept my eyes peeled for trouble.

I panhandled daily at the strip mall in Brooklyn, which most people found to be an eyesore—it had seen better days. We all had. Shoppers wore hoodies and sweats, t-shirts and skating sneakers fleeced for pennies to the dollar.

Sitting on the sidewalk outside an old shoe store, I waited for generous shoppers to flip a coin into my pan. Sometimes, they would miss, and the coin would rattle into the drain, but I wouldn't rebuke them for it. Wouldn't even look at them or say anything. Instead, I had my back against the wall chewing a stalk of grass, pretending at the very least that I had a cigarette, trying to imagine the sweet, toxic delicacy of nicotine and carbon monoxide poisoning speeding up the process of dying. The strip mall was simply a lookout point, somewhere I could hang out and use as a home base when I made transactions to sell items I'd looted—a cover.

I wore a faded t-shirt and a worn-out pair of jeans in the summers, and topped the look with a baseball cap crusted with years of dust and crud.

In the winter, I would wear the same shirt and jeans with an old denim jacket I purchased for a dollar. It was torn at the seams, and old machine oil still clung to its pockets. Several years of rain didn't wash away the stains. Instead, the rain added to the saturation of grime. I had a flannel, too, when winters were particularly harsh.

Mac often came by to check on me here, being one of the few people in the city I spoke to. He counseled me on one occasion. "Everybody needs somebody. You may have lost your friends and family, but it doesn't mean you're alone."

I asked him if he had one—a family, a support system.

"No, Mindo. I have the suppliers. My gang is my family, but they don't look out for me either. I have to look out for myself. It's a different story for you, being a user, you know?"

"How different?"

He eyed me carefully, then smiled like he agreed. "Maybe we're not so different, you and I. You could get into this one day—be a dealer yourself."

I hushed, and he left me alone.

Sitting outside the shoe store, I would daydream about things lurking in the shadows, behind steel fences and concrete garrisons. I would hear slow, plodding footsteps in the dark. Like Romero's zombies in *Night of the Living Dead*. The poor pushed their shopping carts full of scavenged objects while druggies loitered the bridges and docks by the Hudson, snorting crack, injecting vials of fentanyl into decaying cells.

The next day, I was back at the strip mall, pretending to panhandle again. I brought my anatomy textbook and scanned through the images. The diagrams had sectioned-off images of body parts, identified by names and numbers. The numbers corresponded to pages where each function was specified and explained. I skimmed pages to examine the parts of the brain. Hypothalamus, cerebral cortex, pineal gland, and others. I read what each did. Couldn't figure out why the zombies in Tondo didn't die unless there was significant brain damage. Mama and

Papa were shot in the head and died instantly. Doctor Amorsolo fell from the third floor of Tondo General Hospital, but his head managed to survive the fall intact. The result: he spasmed like an electrocuted man but got up like nothing happened. So there had to be an explanation. Some zombies also died when they were unable to feed over time, causing their numbers to dwindle. It was confusing. Governments were not being forthcoming either.

There was little to do but scour for food, scavenge for stuff to sell, buy drugs, or read. It was just like life in Tondo years ago. Except for the drugs.

Still, the zombie phenomenon overseas was worse than any poverty domestically. Minor incidents arose in the country after discoveries of zombies were neutralized by the military and police. Always, the outbreak was prevented. The greater problem was ignored. Meanwhile, the United States population worried about the economic outlook, or the fact that climate change was destroying many cities. Despite great worry that the outbreak would land on U.S. shores, people focused on the prices of commodities, or the U.S. dollar losing even more purchasing power. Since people couldn't afford things—food, shelter, electricity—basic necessities prevailed over the threat of the zombie pandemic's imminent second wave. And because of this economic downtrend, the rise in drug use became a major issue, even though the zombie apocalypse worldwide had been blamed on drugs.

It started with addiction. Then via the infection of a bite. No one could explain it. Despite desperate governments launching preemptive strikes by killing addicts and citizens wounded by zombie outbreaks, other countries couldn't battle the overwhelming numbers of infected cases. In the end, they were eradicating people. Mass graves by the tens of thousands, hundreds of thousands, millions. The borders were closed to prevent the spread of the contagion to U.S. territories. Asylum seekers were denied entry. American immigrants lost their loved ones in foreign countries. In the Philippines, the zombie phenomenon was managed by sedition. The zombies were killed, simple. There was no cure. It seemed that past issues with population density were resolving themselves with violence and extinction via infection.

Memories were tough to bear at night. I had a lifetime to think about, and a lifetime more to live. There was more pain in store, more pain to forget.

My thoughts drifted to my childhood. Where else would I look for old wounds? For scabs to rip open, knowing they would never heal.

Some memories lingered painfully—memories of Mama, Papa, Bodjie, Laleng, Enrico, Jason, Captain Ruiz, and others. Then, when my eyes watered and my heart ached until I could no longer bear it, I'd pump my arm full of heroin and drift into sweet oblivion.

Those memories didn't transition into dreamless, catatonic highs. The drugs numbed the pain by ridding the heart of the worst emotions, reverting thoughts to a blank slate, static and empty, free as opposed to imprisoned.

A conversation with an addiction psychiatrist yielded the following reaction: "The reason illegal drugs are so popular to people from all walks of life is because it treats deficits differently from legal drugs. Besides the substantially more harmful side-effects—addiction, nervous system damage, skin disorders, other serious health problems—it principally does one thing well, and for this reason, manages to survive decades of eradication by the Drug Enforcement Agency and police: it helps people forget. Forget who they were, forget their problems, forget that searching for meaningful ways to cope is difficult. It brings a high not quite mistakable for true happiness. If people wanted to forget something too shameful, too heartbreaking, too painful, too hurtful… They turned to drugs, sex, alcohol, buying, gambling."

The addiction psychiatrist was right. Mac was right. Whatever scratched the itch brought temporary gratification, although it never lasted long enough. The effects of illegal drugs brought results that many suffering, mentally-ill individuals preferred over the struggle of recovery offered by prescription medicines. Medical textbooks described the disease as pathological; it was why addiction psychiatry existed. Workaholics wanted to forget the prospect of failure. Caffeine addicts wanted to forget their lack of exercise and proper diet. A euphoric high was a more certain remedy to preemptively negate the downward spiral. Nobody took drugs knowingly to be happy; it was the opposite—they didn't want to be miserable anymore.

Mac told me the latter part was true. "Killing time means killing pain," he said like a businessman. "This is modern-day New York City. All the gentrification going on post-new millennia swung back full circle when the economy collapsed. Rent has become too steep. Ownership is even worse. The dead housing market is enormous. Inflation has skyrocketed. People don't worry about retirement plans when their money's dry. They go to the funny farm…the pharmacy, I mean. Me."

I ruminated in the sewers and read books like a Ph.D. student, trying to uncover the truth regarding my affliction. Try as I might, my significant trauma couldn't be easily foreshadowed by any dawning of realization. Becoming philosophically inclined didn't change my habits as a drug addict; it didn't cause a radical shift in thinking.

In retrospect, I attempted to ennoble myself with learning; learning through self-help books and not solely those of fiction. In the end, however, I wanted what the drugs gave me. I wanted to forget.

Forget when it was impossible to do so.

CHAPTER 11

DRUG WAR WORLDWIDE

O ver time, the wired fences watching the perimeters of abandoned industrial yards got old, so yes, we climbed them all. Beyond curlicues of iron, deep in a labyrinth of passageways where dead ends were hard to escape, a gang of thugs could have tracked me down in a heart-stopping moment, and I could have ended up dead.

All those years as a child, going to school, obeying my parents, hatching dreams to be a doctor and raising my family out of poverty, I had known better than to take drugs. When life went downhill, when circumstances grew extreme beyond all means to cope, when stress became defiant of all hopes and dreams, I yielded. What changed? What made me turn to the very poison that ended the lives of my loved ones?

Maybe I didn't have the courage to get a gun and pull the trigger. Maybe I wanted to forget, but hadn't been lucky enough to suffer from amnesia.

My instincts were still triggered by the worse situations, no matter how much easier death made things. I remembered Mama and Papa's peaceful faces the day the policeman shot them both, no longer zombies, no longer trapped in bodies transformed beyond cure. I recalled

Captain Ruiz's face on the ship before he pulled the lever, his smile warm and golden, the last time I would see a countryman regard me with that sort of kindness.

I couldn't believe that I was still scavenging. Couldn't believe that I was still hunting for loose change in Coney Island. That I hadn't pumped enough heroin and fentanyl into my veins to permanently rid me of disease and despair and reunite me with my loved ones. Not even when fentanyl made heroin doubly dangerous, two hits close to summoning the dreaded death rattle. Wasn't that what I wanted? Why did I choose a slow death? A slow suicide? In the end, wasn't that more painful?

If I wanted to survive the zombie pandemic, I had to get off drugs before the strain somehow reached U.S. borders. I was ineligible for deportation now that all flights to my country had been grounded years ago.

I even decided to enter AA and rehab, with no success.

The city's Behavioral Health Center was where I sought help for my substance abuse problems. I came weekly after going to a twenty-eight-day program specifically for juvenile delinquents, and saw my counselor every Friday for the first eight weeks before I was finally willing to work hard to get sober. Some attributed this dawning of realization to the success of mandates imposed by a revamped statewide mental health system. The rehab process was actually smeared with controversy. Drug addiction was a business. There were treatment centers, rehabilitation homes, and drug dealers in close proximity of each other. Places like Del Ray Beach in Florida were revolving doors for kids across the country to recycle through treatment and eventually end in overdose. I wanted out of the system; so did most addicts. It became my only motivation. But as soon as I was reassigned to another counselor and I got the run-around from staff at the treatment center, or when life stressors remained too overpowering, I stopped attending AA and counseling altogether.

I didn't go to another doctor. Didn't reenter the broken system just to fall through the cracks again. Didn't end up in better neighborhoods, in shelters, or even on park benches.

I returned to the sewers. Below. That was home. Abandoned subways and tunnels where teens and geriatrics fought for spare change and soda bottles. Mac would be waiting by the subway stations, smiling at me like he knew.

Suffering was the norm. My unfortunate past led to an even worse-than-foreseeable future, but every day was yet another. Another night in a shelter or in my sleeping bag in the sewers stretching into perpetual winter, where death was busy harvesting souls. Another day scouring trash bins across the city, searching for things thrown away by mistake. Another night looting a store before pawning the goods for a quick buck.

I didn't search for help elsewhere. AA meetings in churches. Nicotine patches. Seminars and talks hosted by heroin survivors. I went on with my life. Needless to say, that life was shortening. But what choice did I have? Everyone was doing the same things I did. What was the point?

The AA counselor had so many people on his caseload, it stopped being a choice to help people, and instead became a job. He would speak into a microphone to address the crowd. "Taking drugs is a choice. For most of you, poverty isn't. If you take drugs to cope with poverty, you forfeit the choice to cope with poverty the best you can. Mental illness is real. You're coming here to cope with mental illness, so start there. Take treatment seriously and live to fight another day."

Live to fight? These people were fentanyl addicts and had lost all will to fight. Scarred, broken, defeated, now turned into a cash-cow, my case was a number in a file cabinet or database that spanned millions. I was a face in the crowd, an ant in the anthill right after the death of the queen.

The social security system was bankrupt, and food stamps were being phased out in favor of soup kitchens funded by non-profit organizations.

The lines were outrageously long but people queued up for blocks, for miles, waiting for soup and a stale piece of toast. Scavenging brought far too little money to eat; in America, scrounging for trash didn't earn you a keep. Maybe I would get lucky and haul a decent item I could resell for a good chunk of change. Maybe I would pickpocket a well-dressed dude in the subways and come away with more than a hundred bucks. Maybe I would loot a convenience store and trade candy bars to hungry underground residents in exchange for a small stash. Wherever the means may have been, that's where I looked.

AA counselors belted out the same sermons, the same quotes over and over.

"One day at a time."

"Humility is not thinking less of yourself, but thinking of yourself less."

"If you want what you've never had, you must do what you've never done."

I nodded like an attentive student, but when I rejoined the throngs of impoverished New Yorkers under the city, I capitulated.

Misinterpreted, it all sounded so simple to the alcoholic falling off the wagon.

What's one day drinking? I simply won't drink the next day.

If you think of yourself less, you become less concerned with the results of your actions.

If you'd never had drugs before, why refrain from trying? The thoughts circled in my head and, eventually, my persistence failed.

One day, I fell off the wagon. Distraught, disillusioned with all the words of wisdom I'd retained from self-help books, group therapy discussions, and any pamphlets or handouts, I drank to excess; I got wasted. Then I met Mac in the sewers, and he smiled like a long-lost friend. So why did some AA vets refer to alcohol addiction as one's love at the bottom of a bottle? The clinicians and AA people described it as pathological, but the love of the drink had little to do with what they say makes the disease inevitable—genetics, stress, sexual fulfillment.

The same could be said for drug addiction.

My conclusion: when the will to live has seeped out of all mitochondria, taking drugs and alcohol were the only humane things I could do for myself.

After AA meetings and twelve-step programs became a thing of the past, it was back to panhandling at the broken-down strip mall. I started from being a skinny druggie with prominent elbows and knuckles to looking like a stick figure with a spotted face. I was in so deep with heroin that I was forced to shoot up in my hands or feet.

When I walked the streets, other junkies crowded the walkways, even getting in front of a taxicab blaring its horn. Major cities like New York, Philadelphia, and Seattle became big draws similar to the phenomenon known in Brazil as "Cracolandia," where drug addicts loitered in the streets of a ghetto in Sao Paulo stretching for several blocks. It was as if George A. Romero's *Dawn of the Dead* was happening everywhere.

Some men snorted crack cocaine out in the open. Some kids preferred heroin, numbing their pain beneath sterile dreams. Some women peddled for their next fix. Teens shared a supply of fentanyl pills, then moved on to other crowds to share with theirs so they wouldn't go low so quickly. Since the year 2027 was impending death, famine, and devastation, people didn't need to process everything that was happening because it was all happening too fast. Everyone just wanted to die a slow death, or maybe a quick one. Suicide rates were as high as murder rates in Oakland or St. Louis. Homes were literally decorated with gunshot holes and bloodstains. Drug overdose statistics were off the charts, gurneys lined wall to wall at toxicology departments in city morgues.

There might have been valuables left behind in the homes of the recently deceased. Either that, or I would stay for a while. Almost always, more gangs and looters pushed us out. Abandoned sites were warzones sometimes. People came and went like it was disputed territory. Often, they went in body bags.

———— • ————

I visited Melanie at her spot in the underground tunnels again.

"Are you running from the law?" I asked her.

"What do you mean?"

"You ought to move some place safer. Like to a small town or something. In the country."

"I killed someone," she said.

My eyes held hers. "It doesn't matter now, Melanie. The cops don't give a damn."

"People will find out. They'll think I'm a threat."

"What happened?"

"I killed a man who tried to rape me."

Jenny started crying some. Melanie hushed her, rocked her against her chest.

"New York City is no place for a single parent and a baby. Look around."

"Yeah. Don't you think I've noticed, Mindo? It's shit!"

"Please move on…before it's too late."

"Mindo, do you think they'll let me in one of those sanctuaries they're building, huh? No way! I don't have cash or assets."

"You can live in the country where it's safer. Maybe you'll survive."

She looked at me intently. She was thinking about it.

"Maybe Jenny will survive."

Her eyes glistened. Tears welled. "Okay," she said. "I'll give it some thought. I'll look for a place."

"Good. There's hope for some of us."

She appeared to swallow hard. "Some of us? What about you, Mindo? Where will you go?"

I looked at the walls of the sewer, listened to the sewage flow, stifled tears I had spent a lifetime holding back.

"Nowhere," I said. "This is where it ends for me. Below."

On the street or in the shelters, kids were farmed for their healthy organs, their plasma, their bone marrow. They left them hollow. Or they died of hunger.

Many impoverished teens doubled as prostitutes. Lots of junkies whored for their fix. Riots erupted in Times Square, where the old electronic billboards now displayed porn ads. The scene of Macy's parades and New Year's specials on TV, Times Square returned to being a red-light district reminiscent of *Blade Runner* movies. There were small alleys a short walk from these Cracolandia-like marketplaces where men gangbanged teen girls desperate for money. Seedy motels popped up everywhere, the old broadcasting networks had made way for rental space on the cheap. Gone was NBC and *The Today Show* on Rockefeller Center.

The shrinking numbers of police departments nationwide served the affluent minority, generally disregarding most of the assault and battery cases throughout the city. New York City was surrounded by other towns known for the highest number of murder cases per square mile: Newark and Trenton down south, Albany and Buffalo up north.

Again, Mac offered insight. "Doors made of reinforced steel, almost like bank vaults, with massive bolt locks and chains, have been put in place of flimsy wooden ones. Armed guards and pit bulls are guarding waterfront properties full of debt collateral—expensive cars, expensive equipment, or high-end goods left behind by the economic collapse. If it's expensive, it's there, you name it! The entrances and windows of skyscrapers across Manhattan have been sealed off with steel doors and huge padlocks. Electric wire fences are protecting pricier real estate across the city; these buildings are empty monoliths of stone and marble, monuments to a time rapidly disintegrating." He described it like a museum curator.

Shanties were erected on the Hudson, from New York City all the way to Englewood Cliffs—I even briefly thought about setting up there, but the violence was off the charts. The shanties were made of cardboard, old billboard signs, and industrial garbage like our own slums in Tondo. New York City was now an early millennium third-world ghetto. Pollution entered the Hudson Bay at increasing amounts. Trash would wash ashore on Liberty Island.

Mac was playing some '90s old-school hip-hop from his Bluetooth boombox one day, waiting on a bench in the park for customers. I got the skinny on the fentanyl overdose relevance. "Fentanyl is a hundred times more potent than morphine, my friend," he said like a professor, gesticulating like a hip-hop entrepreneur in contrast. "This makes it much more effective in less time, causing users to pass out high after the point of injection. This is what caused the fentanyl epidemic, which remained a relevant cause of death many years after the initial findings post-millennia. Not making this up. This drug started a revolution," he said to me, like fentanyl did addicts more good than harm.

I thought about the consequences. If true, and a biological weapon was inserted into the illegal drug supply in Asia, Central and South America, and Africa, then the infusion of synthetic fentanyl in heroin might have been poised to infect people outright, not transform them into hordes of bloodthirsty zombies slowly.

Mac dished yet another story. "I did some digging, Mindo. Google scholar articles describing fentanyl's history, like a Dr. Theodore H.

Stanley from the University of Utah Health Sciences Center in Salt Lake City, gave a history of fentanyl's development in a research article, describing the drug's earliest beginnings in Belgium in the 1950s by Janssen Pharmaceutica to address the need for a more effective perioperative opioid analgesic. The latter term is just scientific lingo for surgical anesthesia."

Now, this was where the explanation got difficult. My interview subject went on. "During World War Two, after fentanyl's performance as a rapid presentation, short-term efficacy palliative made it popular for many types of surgery and pain management, the supply of fentanyl in the market exploded after the Food and Drug Authority approved its use for mass consumption. This just means that after the drug exceeded expectations as a short-lasting, quick-acting anesthetic, the FDA approved the drug for anybody to get their hands on."

I nearly cringed. *This is how drugs end up in Mac's hands to sell to the public?*

He shifted on his seat as he continued. "Some of this stuff is still online. If you can't search them all, there's a collection of articles and videos on a darknet site called armageddonnet, accessible through Tor."

He continued with his elaborate explanations. "Other Google scholar articles describe statewide investigations into the overdosing trends, as well as toxicology reports stating that even more fentanyl was cut into past heroin supplies than ever before. After studies performed between 2014 and 2016 in states such as Massachusetts, Maine, our very own New York State, and Ohio by the Drug Enforcement Agency showed a one-hundred-fifty percent increase in fentanyl-related overdose deaths as a result of the mixture of fentanyl into the illegal drug supply, the new fentanyl epidemic became a spotlight of media scrutiny and government oversight. It also gave us a routine blank check," Mac said. "To make matters worse, when a synthetic fentanyl called carfentanil, that was one thousand times more potent than morphine, was eventually popularized as the fentanyl of choice in the illegal drug trade, the percentages of overdose deaths during 2020 to 2027 rose by a rate of three hundred fucking percent."

Mac looked at me then. "While it's obvious, Min, that fentanyl and carfentanil mixing into the heroin and crack cocaine supply was causing deaths, people were also mixing dangerously and taking too much, spiking those trends by alarming degrees."

Mac explained it all like a statistician. Methodical. Emotionless.

I asked him what he used to do before selling drugs, and he said he worked in a chemical manufacturing plant. I didn't know what to tell him, being an addict, other than, "That's fascinating," before crossing my arms against my chest like the information overload was encouraging.

"It doesn't end there," he said. "These findings showed a rapid increase in carfentanil mixing with other opioids in the late 2000s, stemming the rapid surge of deaths for seven years from 2020 onward. The illegal drug trade was no longer interested in keeping users around for years to milk them of their assets. These carfentanil-based drugs were relatively cheap and produced a dramatically intensified high that was addictive with only one take. It meant the end of casual users who sporadically took drugs for parties. It meant that anyone taking the drug was hooked instantly. Users who were in-deep were thrice more susceptible to potentially fatal overdoses. Users who sold stash knew how to cut small doses, spread them out, and tolerate some of the lows to survive. The alternative was blowing six cuts in one take and overdosing before anyone could apply mouth to mouth and several doses of Naloxone," he said, like he was completely oblivious to the fact that he sold the stuff.

I'd survived for seven years because I never cut too much into one dosage. Just did enough to kill the pain, forget Mama and Papa's faces, forget Captain Ruiz's last smile, forget the sight of Laleng's corpse feasted on by zombies, or Jason crying out in pain as he was devoured alive. I didn't want to die. I was scared. What was wrong with me? Why couldn't I cut enough carfentanil into the mix to stop my breathing? I took drugs by myself. No one would save the day with three or four doses of Naloxone to revive me. Tears streamed down my face whenever I took my switchblade out and placed it against my wrist. Just another day.

Rumors about the biological weapon were still unconfirmed. It was the strongest theory devisable. A country had yet to emerge as the rightful claimant to the mystery of the drug's origin. Experts in health departments worldwide suggested that chemical agents in Asia, Central and South America, and Africa were injected into the meth supply. It was consistent. The cheapest meth variant in the Philippines, *shabu*, was dubbed a high-risk for this deadly chemical compound. Pharmaceutical companies around the world were researching the effects of these drugs on mice.

Mac took out his smartphone and showed me a video of a mouse in a cage, sourced from a pharmaceutical laboratory, showing the animal convulse in a seizure before attacking other mice. The mouse's eyes were crimson; its veins had darkened blue-black; its muscles spasmed. After it bit one mouse and then another, the other mice turned bloodthirsty too. Soon, the whole cage was filled with wild, convulsing, red-eyed mice making harsh, shrill noises. The lab technician used tongs to lower a chicken leg, and they devoured it like piranhas.

Mac smiled as the video ended and offered his own opinion. "I'm used to getting a blank check by now, but something tells me I'll have to get a new job soon."

I couldn't agree more.

CHAPTER 12

A New Beginning. A New End

Violence was on the upswing. Boarded-up windows shielded hostile environs inside. At night, the quarrels spilled to the streets, frequently lasting until dawn. White gangs and Black gangs fought in Union Square, blood staining the sidewalks. Men standing on corners or outside stores were gunned down at all hours. Alleys and side streets were home to stick fights where switchblades and jackknives reigned supreme.

I knew better than to stay. But I did.

Mac was hanging out on Broadway, at a street corner close to a brothel that used to be a theater, sitting on a bench close to the traffic light.

This time, he offered to take me in. "The money's good," he said.

I told him I didn't trust myself with the merchandise. "I'd blow it all in one take." It was a lie. I didn't want to sell drugs. Had promised Mama and Papa I wouldn't. Maybe I'd promised Bodjie.

"Takes dedication," he said, seemingly proud of his token vocation. "Selling drugs isn't quite as bad as people make it out to be. Buyers create demand. Without buyers, there wouldn't be dealers. Without a market, there wouldn't be supply."

Here I am. Still around. Still his guinea pig.

I remembered what I'd once told Bodjie: *You know, stay in school; your future is on the line.*

But Bodjie was gone.

People in NYC had no long-term future, no dreams. Just the next day...if we made it. Just pain driving us to our knees, driving us to insanity.

Mama and Papa's words came to me again. "*Ipangako mo,*" Mama had said. *Promise us... Promise you won't take drugs.*

Then I remembered what Bodjie had turned into. What Enrico turned into. And how Mama, Papa, and Doctor Amorsolo had not survived.

I bought drugs anyway. Life was all too much to take. All your friends, your family, gone. Dead. They had died such horrible deaths, and I had survived. Had lived to see another day and watched the world inch slowly toward its demise.

"Got me a stash?" I told Mac, looking behind him at some girls coming out of the brothel. He sold drugs to little kids too, sometimes— young Black kids who needed a way out of life. His clients lived in tenements by the bay, underground in the subways, or in the Bronx where some apartment buildings were like the housing projects of the nineties. Typically, Mac's customers didn't survive to twenty-one years of age.

"I do if you got my money," he said.

I gave him a low five and a smile. Mac was an unusual name for a Black kid. I always thought that it was a typical white man's name.

"What's going down?" I asked him, trying to play homie. I treated him like a friend. Like Bodjie, Jason, Enrico, or Laleng. To me, he was the pharmacy. No prescriptions necessary. To him, I was the friendly customer. I was reliable. A regular, which meant I was a steady source of income. I was an investment.

Until I ended up dead.

"Yo, you got to check it out," he said excitedly. "My homies found a body on a bench in the middle of Central Park...in the middle of Central fuckin' Park, man. I mean, in the middle of the day. They thought he was free-wheeling—whoring or dealing in someone else's territory."

I reached into my wallet, handed him the cash, and made the exchange—I stuffed the little plastic packet with white powder in my coat pocket. When placed in a syringe and injected into a vein, it was mass-marketed heaven on earth.

"Yo," he said, gesticulating. "He was from below, like you. He wasn't shot, beaten, or stabbed…"

"What you sayin'?" I asked, suddenly interested.

"He was eaten."

I knew right away this was the beginning of the end.

Again.

Mac was right.

Bodies started showing up everywhere—out in the open, in cardboard boxes, in warehouses-turned-shelters, in abandoned buildings, and in housing projects. People were dying in increasing numbers. Was it gun violence? Violent crime? Everyone's answer? Yes. But I couldn't forget what Mac had said: someone had been eaten and left in Central Park. Eaten by what? Cannibals? Like in Tondo a lifetime ago? Zombies? Bodjie and Enrico, and later my papa, after being bitten by another infected person? Governments had sanctioned their military and police to shoot infected people, the zombies, as well as the victims they wounded to prevent the spread of infection. The United States closed its borders a short time later to quarantine against the pandemic. If the zombie phenomenon had first started from persons taking cheap, synthetic drugs—as speculated—governments eventually cracked down on cartels and drug lords by tightening borders and cutting off distribution. They also waged full-scale wars on those cartels and their supply chain, which was something governments never took much interest in to end the drug problem worldwide in the nineties and early 2000s.

However, the plan was merely a desperate pre-emptive strike to prevent supply of dirty chemical compounds or biological weapons from reaching first-world countries. The damage to the economy was the greatest factor in the demand for more supply of drugs. Once lives were ruined, and more and more people were driven to extreme lengths of difficulty and tragedy, the more people craved a means to cope. Therapy was too expensive. Psychiatric medicine was too. The easiest, most effective means to numb the perilous longing to end all suffering and hardship was opioid-based drugs.

It started with cheap meth in poor countries like the Philippines, something to make you feel alive. Now, the new drug of choice was heroin. Its cousins were also in demand: crack cocaine and morphine, drugs that helped you forget, for hours at a time, that life was too hard.

But fentanyl-based heroin would trump them all. What if a fentanyl-based biological weapon was used to cut into the supply of heroin, and what if carfentanil was used? There would be no gradual transformation into a zombie state. It would be instant and deadly.

A new frontier was emerging in the drug trade, namely xylazine, also called tranq, an animal tranquilizer used to slow breathing and the heart rate, besides lowering blood pressure. If carfentanil was much too deadly, xylazine would be a safer replacement. Perhaps it would prove more stable, so dealers could hook addicts longer to milk them of their assets. Due to the horror of first-usage mortalities that carfentanil was causing, xylazine was becoming a safer alternative.

If the chemical compounds in *shabu* were likewise found in new supplies of heroin and crack cocaine, then the zombie phenomenon had truly made its way to New York City.

The images popped up on TV. I didn't have one, so I relied on my smartphone. I bought data from a vendor, something popular in third-world countries before the United States also fell poor.

Bodies were found all over the city—some rotting, some lying in gutters in plain sight, and others lining the alleys and slums along the Hudson.

The bodies that particularly drew my interest were mysteriously eaten. Feral animals could have been the culprits. Or the same could have been caused by sewer rats, populations of which had exploded in the city and the underground tunnels. In fact, I made company down below with roaches and rodents. The theory was plausible.

What was looking likelier was that people were eating these bodies.

There were no rampaging hordes of zombies. Nothing like Tondo. Where were these new strains coming from? Where were they hiding?

News stations would focus coverage on all the dead bodies. New York City was no longer safe. City employees in white suits sprayed disinfectant on contaminated areas. New York was becoming a mass grave. The Macy's and the Bloomingdales were all shut down to make room for tents and camps within the mall, lined up wall-to-wall with people in beanies, puff jackets, and fleece sweaters huddling around fires while staring blankly at TVs. News reporters predicted an outbreak in the United States much worse than the bubonic plague and coronavirus pandemics from years past.

Or worse than the zombie pandemic in Asia. Worse than what I experienced in the Philippines.

I broke into the New York City Public Library through the sewers. Inside, I took one book from the shelf, took another, said wow, and took the next. I couldn't decide what to read. I was the scholarly kid from Tondo who learned to read to cure the blues. Books and heroin. The latter was a grave mistake. But the damage was done.

I read more medical books. Also read up on pharmacology. About snake venom entering the blood stream via a bite and crippling someone's heart. I read books that described a human brain's neurons releasing dopamine after cardio-pulmonary arrest, triggering an experience similar to dreaming just before true death. But in the end, I needed to interview someone. There were experts from all over the world doing clinical trials to isolate the effects of the new drugs on the human brain. They were collecting brain tissue samples from dead zombies. The news reports said the brains had completely decayed though. Did that mean they eventually rotted after being deprived of blood or meat consumption? Was that what caused the zombie populations overseas to thin out over time? I wanted to sate my curiosity. Perhaps test my theory. My dreams of working in medicine or research had faded, but had not died.

It was hard to see in the library, hard to read. The windows were boarded up, so it was dark. Felt claustrophobic. I had to take breaks because I didn't want to drastically impair my eyesight, although it might have been a lost cause. My pupils were clouding, and the sclera were yellowing with jaundice. My arms had so many needle marks due to abscess that they were crippling my hand movements, and might have been infected all the way to the bone by now. The staff at the drug treatment center had told me that a blood transfusion would be necessary in such cases. I didn't have money for antibiotics and treatment anyway. So, yes, I had to stay. Nay, I was stuck in America where the pandemic was now entering a second wave.

I left the library the same way I entered, certain the answers didn't lie there. I just didn't know where to find them.

Back at my home in the sewers, eating some stale toast and old deli leftovers, I decided to beeline to Melanie's spot to check if she had eaten that day. I found her holding Jenny, as usual, but she seemed to be frustrated because Jenny was crying and wouldn't stop.

"I think she's sick, Mindo. I have to climb up to an infirmary, get her medical attention."

I nodded, handed Melanie the piece of bread I'd sneaked out of the soup kitchen in addition to mine. We started climbing to the streets, talking.

"I think she got bitten by a rat here in the sewers. When I heard her crying, I picked her up and tried to breastfeed her, and she bit my nipple. I mean, ouch!"

I didn't have a clue what to say. "Just get her to the doctor," I told her. "Are you going to be okay, Melanie?"

"Yeah, I'm fine. I think. I found a small town north of here. In Vermont. Low incidences of drug abuse and crime. I'm planning to head there."

She ate the piece of bread on the way out of the sewers with me. Then she told me she would head to Cedars Sinai Hospital Emergency Room to get Jenny seen.

"I'll be back to say goodbye," she said.

I watched her leave. Melanie held Jenny close, and still, the baby didn't stop crying. I had a bad feeling, but headed over to an art collective at the waterfront to visit my only other friend in the city. I needed to clear my head.

Gaia was a painter, and had lost her apartment when the recession turned ugly and spiraled into this Second Great Depression that'd brought the city to its knees.

Gaia translated to "life" or "earth" in Greek mythology, but she didn't look like it. She looked like a goth in her black faux leather, black fishnets, black lipstick, black everything. Gaia should have changed her name to *Death*. Her art would have agreed.

I'd thought about hitting her up for dates many times, but I wasn't crazy. She loved hanging out with me, and as long as she welcomed me to her cliquish social circle, hope sprang eternal.

She wasn't typically into guys from below, but I got it. Who would be? Still, I occasionally shared my booze, so she dug me. You could tell by her smile. She was that type, sincere. Didn't play pretend and then look as obvious as a clown in a circus.

Gaia used to see a big-wig artist who moved down south to a walled community in Georgia to escape the violence and harsh winters. When he left, so did her financial security. Gaia had talent, so she could easily join a collective and bunk with a bunch of other NYU standout artists.

Like I said, the other artists easily let me in because they knew me. I found Gaia's bunk in a corner of the warehouse where she was busy sketching, and she held it up for my inspection.

"Fascinating," I said to her. It was a sketch of a corpse surrounded by vagrants. The corpse's eyes were missing, and the oval mouth indicated that the person had screamed in agony during its death throes.

"Thanks, bud," she said, smiling like a nuclear winter hadn't descended upon us all. "Things are moving. Art buyers upstate can't wait for more corpse art," she said, winking.

"Of course," I said, knowing she wouldn't have it any other way. I noticed how she called me "bud," like we were homies, and I retracted a little. I had a crush on her. The other artists would whisper things, how I wanted to get into her panties and all.

Gaia reminded me of Laleng, who was good at arts and crafts, even though Laleng wanted to work as a nurse. Gaia was an American version perhaps.

"Say…" she said, stammering. "I noticed that your eyes were yellow. You also look horribly emaciated. What gives?"

I didn't know what to tell her. I remembered Mama, Papa, Bodjie, Enrico, and Doctor Amorsolo. Yes, I was a junkie. No, I didn't want to die. If and when the second wave of the pandemic would hit New York City from the contaminated fentanyl supply, I would likely get infected. Become a zombie too. Somebody had to be kind enough. Aim for the head and not hesitate.

I shrugged. "Must be the drugs and thug life," I said with a smile.

147

She laughed like she didn't buy it.

"By the way," I said while checking out her collection of corpse art. "Did you get up close to a body to paint it, or I mean, sketch it?"

She grinned even wider now, her cheekbones almost like razors under her pale skin. "Want to learn art, Min? Want to see how it's done?"

I didn't. But I didn't know what else to do in a city that sleeps with one eye open. I guess what I wanted was the grand tour: bodies in warehouses fresh from death via overdosing, bodies with mortal wounds—maybe missing parts of the anatomy, like the liver, the heart, the brain. I didn't know. After a lifetime of violence, I didn't know what else to do, how else to pass the time until my own violent death took me.

"I'll show you," she said. "My Uncle Morgan is a pathologist. That's where I go to find models for my work."

————— ◈ —————

I'd heard wild tales of laboratory contractors kidnapping homeless persons to harvest healthy tissue for a quick buck. I'd seen homeless people volunteer for experiments to get cash before dying of complications and overdoses on the merciless streets. But I didn't think I'd find makeshift morgues and mortuaries underground.

Gaia led me to her uncle's mortuary in an abandoned subway tunnel, in a section closed off by a dead end. Bodies on top of gurneys lined each wall, stretching several blocks under the city. The chill down there during winter helped preserve the bodies.

"My," I said, "this is some freezer."

Gaia gave me a look over and smiled. Her uncle wasn't home, and she had unfettered access to his mortuary royale—her own art studio. "I know it stinks down here, but you must be used to it. Below isn't the Waldorf Astoria."

The Waldorf had seen better days since New York City's affluent locals fled north to the valleys. It was an infirmary now.

"I live down in the sewers, not in the subways, so my place is worse. The stench does make my stomach turn though. This is still gross, by all means."

We uncovered a body, and the bloated corpse had bite marks along the arms and legs. It blew my mind. News stations were saying that rat populations were skyrocketing. But what were they eating?

Gaia had an idea. "The rats like small kids," she said. "Check this one out."

She uncovered a body; the small girl looked half-devoured—face, fingers, toes, excised sections of the shoulders and thighs, like something took big bites.

"What did I tell you?"

"Those aren't rat bites, Gaia. They look like human teeth."

She looked at the body again. Frowned. "What are you saying?"

"I'm saying the government is hiding something."

She waved away my words. "I'm going to stay and do some sketches. There's a prestigious art gallery in the Hamptons that needs some paintings."

The hairs on the back of my neck and arms stood up like hundreds of people were staring at us. But it was just Gaia and me...and hundreds of corpses. That last part explained everything.

I checked out a few more bodies while Gaia was busy. More missing chunks. More loose entrails. It all looked like Tondo during the zombie outbreak.

I felt dizzy.

Needed a fix.

I roamed Coney Island, looking for people walking alone, looking for thug-types to bump into and rob blind of their wallets. Other loiterers watched me with hawk eyes, imagining what they'd do to me if they caught me freewheeling.

Ice cream cones littered the waste bins. Trash littered the board-walk. Some waded in the water, washing along the sand and rocks. I checked the waste bins for other loot—things customers might have left behind at booths, where unscrupulous employees might have taken whatever was valuable and discarded the evidence. I found some bags of popcorn and soda cans that weren't empty. Flies buzzed.

Coney Island crawled with junkies dealing and using. *Cracolandia in Coney Island.* What a great headline for a paper. Unfortunately, no one in New York cared anymore. The city was infested with junkies. Apocalypse now!

I remembered Tondo years ago. America quarantined itself from the disaster by cutting off the drug trade from sources like Mexico and the ports. I asked a drug-dealer friend in Coney Island for the scoop. He was a Rasta man wearing athletic gear and dreads. He was happy to tell the tale. "Drugs are made in makeshift laboratories domestically now and distributed by anyone from white biker gangs, to Latino gangs in old El Caminos, to African-American gangs in luxury sedans trying to survive on what they can. Jamaican reefer is old news, I'm afraid. Fentanyl is the new king of the drug trade, man."

Despite drugs becoming more expensive because of the tighter bor-der control, the cartels were getting smarter, using synthetic variants like carfentanil to lace drug supplies. It wasn't imported as contraband across the border, and it was also cheap to make. Hence, the rapid ascent of carfentanil, which was used mostly for horses.

I checked the public restroom to see who was inside, likely dudes in leather coats, passed out drunk on the tiles. Instead, I walked in on some kids who were stooped over the urinals and looked like they were doing dope. I was disgusted; sharing needles and pumping vials full of urine into each other like the near-death experience was a big thrill-seek.

The kids saw me walk in. The eldest looked particularly worried I'd sound alarms. "Want some?" he asked me, pretending to let me in on their fun. He looked haughty, like a private school kid. The others were just his lackeys, content to follow orders like mindless foot soldiers. Kids desperate for acceptance.

"Fuck that," I said to them. "I ain't doing nothing like that, you crazies!"

They must have noticed something strange because they were staring, and had also begun pinching their noses. Instead of shutting my mouth, I turned to the mirror and saw two rows of yellow teeth, my scalloped tongue, and my gingivitis-infected gums turning slick black.

The kids soured. It showed on their faces. I asked the tall kid if they had any hard drugs or cash to give me, and he sounded pissed off.

Then he suddenly brightened up like a kid who'd just seen candy. "Hey, hand yours over!" the kid said to me, gesturing with a fist. "What do you think, boys?" he asked his friends. "Why don't we beat him up and see if he has a stash instead?"

"There's more of me around," I said to them. "Let's see if you can get out of this place alive!"

"Fuck! Let's beat his monkey brains in!" the kid yelled.

I smiled, slipped out of the restroom, and ran for the fences.

They came out in hot pursuit, but they wouldn't have beaten anyone to the races. Plus, I knew Coney Island like the back of my hand. As a thief, I'd managed to make a dash so many times.

I ran in my sneakers like I'd run barefoot on the streets of Tondo. Darted through the wind like my skinny arms were cut-up bat wings, and made for the tents. I knew I would lose them at the rides. There were too many people, too many of my friends looking out for one another.

The punks slowed at the entrance to the merry-go-round and decided to split up. The eldest kid hollered at them to keep up the chase.

Two of them headed for the booths while another two went in the direction of the boardwalk. The eldest kid stayed hot on my tail, taking out a knife while looking out with keen eyes.

He was staking out the roundabouts where the garbage bins were stashed away from customers' eyes, where staffers used to smoke joints and get high while on break. Some of the vagrants cleared out when they saw him approaching, perhaps knowing he was in trouble.

I hid behind a bin that had a great vantage point, and expected some of the vagrants to step in and jump him for loose change. After all, the haughty kid was alone, and he seemed just the type they looked for—dressed like a varsity goon, like Jet and his friends in Tondo.

Then a weird feeling surfaced. The vagrants drew closer. They crawled out of the shadows and surrounded the garbage bins like zombies, encircling the kid. What the fuck was happening?

The druggies pounced on him from behind, but even from where I was, I couldn't get a good look at the fracas. They crowded him while he was on the ground, and I felt the butterflies rip my belly. *What the fuck?*

Two minutes must have passed while I watched the junkies bob their heads until they finally moved away.

The kid lay behind the garbage bin, no longer moving.

I edged out of my hiding place.

Drew closer.

They didn't just beat him.

Mouthfuls of meat were missing from his neck, arms, cheek, and stomach. Some of his organs appeared to be gone: his liver, his heart.

There was so much blood.

I remembered Bodjie and other scavenger zombies eating Laleng and other residents of Happyland.

I screamed.

Screamed and screamed and screamed.

CHAPTER 13

THE END COMPLETE

I slithered back into the shadows and retreated underground, finding my little corner after a long walk smoking a cigarette I'd picked up from the trash.

Curled up in my sleeping bed, I injected some heroin. It was a larger stash, enough for the gang of five kids at Coney Island. I took so much heroin, I nearly kicked the can. Was out like a light for almost twenty hours.

I started hearing sounds coming from behind the wall, like people whispering, like bones on a rope rattling—perhaps a necklace made by an old tribe.

Curiosity had me up and proceeding to the adjacent tunnel. The slow walk was grueling, given the conditions. The water deepened leading into those tunnels, meaning there were more rats swimming, more cockroaches crawling on the walls. My body was still fresh from a near-flatlining. What was out there? What were the rats and roaches trying to get away from? The clicking, roiling sounds around me grew louder, buzzing like the entire tunnel was covered by a swarm.

Seeing the water, I remembered walking down the embankment at Tondo during the outbreak and seeing island shanties like Isla ng Puting Bato flooding from the bay. Power was out. The residents living on the first-floor shanties hadn't evacuated, content to brave conditions while the standing water of up to three feet flooded the interiors of houses. When zombies approached from inland via driftwood and rubber tires, like rats in a sewer, it meant the people of Isla ng Puting Bato would have no escape. At first, they staved off invasion, hitting the zombies on the heads with poles and beams, then cowered in the corners of their homes as the men were overpowered by sheer numbers, screaming their tonsils out while their children were ripped from their grasp.

My mind switched back to the present. I trudged farther down the tunnel to the set of iron bars at the very end. Beyond that… The sight terrified me.

Déjà vu.

Just like in Tondo, under the construction site, this set of bars sealed off a labyrinth of tunnels rarely visited because raw sewage there ran knee-deep.

On the other side of the iron bars was a community of savages—people living in the underground tunnels feeding on rats and bloated corpses. The corpses must have belonged to people from below too, but I wasn't sure. They could have come from the mortuaries, ones just like Uncle Morgan's. I tried hard to get a look at the savages. Their eyes were dulled, cloudy. I shone a flashlight at them, and they shielded their eyes with their haggard arms and clawed hands, making this throaty rasp that sounded anything but human.

"Aaarrrggghhh!"

They might have looked just like the pack of junkies in Coney Island—the ones who ate the haughty kid, but worse. They didn't wear clothes fit for brutal winters. Instead, the material barely clung to bags of skin and bones; the rags were stained by old blood and gore. They had long, dark fingernails, wild frizzy hair, and dark, spotted skin. The blood vessels and sinews along their arms, necks, and shoulders stuck out like leaf veins. The diet of carrion, cadaver meat, and rodent flesh must have transformed their bodies beyond normal human comparison.

Was this version of the zombie phenomenon an effect of heroin's slow, progressive decay and dulling of the senses? *Shabu*-users-turned-addicts in Tondo moved faster; they ate meat from living humans. These zombies lumbered and lurched. They didn't mind eating corpse flesh.

I ran as fast as I could, as far as my tired feet could take me. Left my sleeping bed and my stash of needles in the underground and vowed never to return.

But was it all real? Or was it just the drugs? I took a shit ton of drugs, but I didn't know anymore. I couldn't believe what I'd seen or heard.

The art collective building at the waterfront was cramped, and nothing exciting but art and jamming was taking place there. Sometimes, Gaia and I sat in and listened to the other artists play acoustic rock. Their music was dark: folk Americana popularized by Townes Van Zandt and Leonard Cohen. The artist-types liked their throwback music.

Gaia knew better than to head to places like the Bronx, Coney Island, or other derelict-infested places in New York. She feared getting attacked. Gaia didn't look scared of anyone, even muggers and thieves, but the Cracolandia-like crowds of junkies made her nervous. She didn't tell me, but she hinted that they were progressing into something much, much worse.

"How?" I asked.

She only said, "It's becoming safer below, in the sewers or in the subways."

After I'd seen and heard the savages in the sewers, I feared the worst. But I didn't tell her. I didn't want to believe.

So, Gaia and I visited Uncle Morgan. I found his name fitting for his profession. He was a pathologist, so it had a nice ring to it.

Uncle Morgan greeted us warmly. He shook my hand when Gaia introduced me as her friend; he seemed lenient, and didn't give her a hard time. He was wiry-thin, had hairy arms and an unkempt beard. He reminded me of Salman Rushdie. Home Hidden Home.

"Want to stay with us and help with my work?" he said. "I could use the extra hands."

"Yes," I said, then followed them to the harvest floor.

It was here that Uncle Morgan eviscerated the bodies. Afterward, he cleaned them up and prepped them for their containments. Most bodies weren't even claimed. Some were donated to universities for research while the rest were buried in mass graves or cremated.

The number of bodies on the harvest floor had doubled since my previous visit. Gaia looked like she was in her element, wearing a lab coat, maybe thinking about following in her uncle's footsteps. Uncle Morgan put on his gown, and Gaia pushed a tray full of surgical instruments with us. We were about to get started.

One body needed a brain removed. Uncle Morgan told me he was still checking for cause of death. When he made the incision and used the electric saw to cut through the skull, the body gasped. We stepped back.

Gaia's fear was as stark as my own. The corpse appeared to be alive. But Uncle Morgan explained that it was simply spasming like it wasn't clinically dead, like neurons were firing after the heart had ceased to beat. Was that what the zombies were though? After we stood back and watched the corpse convulse, it collapsed back onto the table and stopped moving. Uncle Morgan made certain it was dead by using a rod to pierce the corpse's neck—no response.

He looked at me calmly as he spoke. "That's normal. The corpses spasm at least once when you try to excise the brain."

Gaia and I nodded. She stood behind me, both of us watching what Uncle Morgan was going to do with the body.

The man lifted the eyelids, and the body didn't flinch. Satisfied, he extracted the brain from the open incision and cut off the stem. Then he placed the brain on a platter to analyze it.

"I suspect that a novel brain disease might have infected this person. Look at the tissue. There are indications of massive cerebral necrosis all over." He probed the tissue with his instruments, incising from the basal ganglia and revealing some recently living tissue. "This indicates that the brain was functional in terms of involuntary muscle movements," he said. "Primal human functioning is engaged here. Eating. Hunting. Nothing more. Like they were cavemen perhaps."

We shared a look.

Had we stumbled onto something?

Sad, skinny, at my wit's end due to the heroin low, I turned on my smartphone and watched the news. Anchorman Steve Broussard's slot was on, where he regularly kept New York residents abreast of the latest developments surrounding the zombie phenomenon.

Broussard had fair hair, blue eyes, a wide oblong face with a smooth complexion. He sounded perfect for an anchorman's job and rarely did investigative reporting. But today, Broussard had never looked more worried. He had to maintain a formality and detachment during his news coverage, but the news was clearly worrisome this time. Coverage showed grisly scenes of junkies moving through the streets, sometimes dive-bombing unsuspecting vagrants lying on sidewalks who couldn't move or otherwise refused to resist.

Broussard spoke. "Good evening, New York City, and the world. Bad news comes to us this morning from the World Health Organization. The WHO reports that the 'Second-Wave Zombie Pandemic' is nearing fever pitch, and cities worldwide are overcrowded, with infected cases reaching the millions. Already, state and local officials suspect tens of millions of cases are sweeping the poorest districts in the nation and across the world. Poorer countries are finding even more difficulty controlling the violence and spread of infection."

The environmental disasters connected to climate change had to be some of the worst backbreakers of modern civilization. With economic disaster following, food scarcity and homelessness were forcing nations toward world war. Now, every country was becoming overrun by zombies?

"These zombies roaming the streets enacting violence may not truly be infected with some alleged novel virus, as speculated," Broussard noted. "Studies are underway to find the cause of the issue, but one scientific researcher claims that these zombie-like crowds have one common denominator: drugs. Dirty street drugs, with unstable chemical compounds made from home laboratories somewhere in the world, could be contaminating the infected person's brain and causing instances of mass cerebral necrosis. As a result, cognitive faculties quickly erode, thereby resulting in the deterioration of normal functioning and the impairment of said person's analytical abilities. Let's bring our guest speaker up and ask him a few questions…"

The guest speaker was an old man wearing glasses and an Oxford coat. He was probably eighty, and didn't look like he was there to blow smoke.

"This is not just some novel virus causing a widespread pandemic," the old man said. "This is a resurgence of cannibalism not seen since the days of tribal violence and primitive man, spurred by abnormalities in brain function as caused by viral encephalopathy or by corrosive chemical compounds found in toxic home-made street drugs. Once infected, the brain experiences almost irreversible degeneration and cerebral infarction, causing spasmodic movements, organ failure, septicemia, and the insatiable urge to hunt down prey."

I gripped my phone tight as he continued.

"These are not technically zombies. At an early stage, I think the damage to the infected person's brain can be reversible. They are not quite living dead. Until the brain has suffered extensive damage via necrosis, the person may still recover and live," the old man said. "There's hope that if we find a cure or vaccine, we can reverse some of the necrosis and infarction, and the person may survive. Neurosurgical procedures have not been successful in combatting the condition thus far.

"These chemical compounds could have been accidentally synthesized in primitive laboratories, or they could have been engineered with the purpose of destroying the world," he concluded.

I turned my phone off, not knowing what to believe. The theories were going to rage for some time until the mysterious ailment could be cured.

Safe below, close to the subway stations this time, joining other vagrant communities, mortuaries, and makeshift surgery centers, I realized I still wasn't safe. Should those savages find us, they could surround us. They moved very slowly like zombies in the old movies, but they crowded you from all angles like Komodo dragons. I decided to check in at hospital charity wards, complaining of an assortment of issues. I slept at warehouse shelters, braving the violence and noise. I even stayed in a boiler room near the waterfront until other vagrants discovered the place and pushed me out.

I went to see Gaia at her Uncle Morgan's mortuary to see if she was busy painting her models. The bodies in the morgue were being feasted on by the savages. The monsters had found the makeshift mortuary, and it was a free-for-all. They hoisted livers, hearts, and strings-of-sausage-link small and large intestines in the air while feeding like prehistoric men and women. While watching the carnage, I caught sight of Uncle Morgan in a lab coat lying on the ground with a crater in his belly, his guts missing, blood everywhere.

Then I found a group of savages stooped over another body. When they cleared the scene, Gaia lay on the ground without eyes, lips, tongue, or breasts. I wondered whether she would have appreciated how she looked right then, whether she would have painted herself that way, her two remaining fingers on her hand guiding the brush to capture her deathly allure on canvas.

I knew it was pointless. Below, in the underground. That was home. I knew I'd return someday. There was no escaping above ground, where the zombies steadily increased in number. They flooded through infirmaries and shelters and waited for nightfall to hunt fresh prey. The Statue of Liberty stood watch over the chaotic city, a zombie on the crown feeding on a watchman as news crews captured footage from helicopters. The Brooklyn Bridge was backed up all the way past Lincoln Tunnel, cars slammed end to end in a pile-on as zombies fed on the stranded motorists.

Although long closed due to the economic collapse, the Museum of Modern Art's fine sculptures mingled with slow-lurching savages. Ticket booths at Grand Central Station were stained red. The trains didn't move; the windows were shattered; the floors were covered with black, soupy bowels. Wall Street was silenced, the trading floor holding space to a massacre, becoming a harvest floor for organs instead.

Cedars Sinai Hospital, the Waldorf Astoria, Radio City Music Hall, and Carnegie Hall were reminiscent of Tondo General Hospital and the C.M. Recto area. Fires raged, burning bodies fell from patios and rooftops, faces and necks burst open with bite wounds, coloring the buildings crimson, while throngs of savages converged on screaming patients and shelter residents, leaving no one alive.

I ended up seeking shelter in the sewers, where the savages might be less prone to venture. But I knew they would come for me. Before long, they would catch up. Their black, rotting teeth would sink into my flesh, clots of gore hanging between the gaps like red ribbons. My flesh, my heart, my brain matter, offerings to the new apex predators. Nature was crying for vengeance. All hail the new species, dying Mother Earth cried in admiration.

Perhaps, even better yet, I'd join them and learn to love the taste of rat flesh, bloated corpses, and living humans. I would wear bones strung on a necklace, cut-off fingers for charms, eyeballs for pendants. Perhaps I would never know life aboveground again, never see the sun, never see the bright lights of New York City, a world at war with reason and a place plunged into darkness and deprivation.

———— ◦ ————

I watched the news from my smartphone down in the sewers the next day, huddling in my sleeping bag from the cold. The next great pandemic—maybe the last one—was here. Steve Broussard was back on the air. The studies were conclusive. The strain of viral encephalopathy that was infecting people through drug use and bite wounds was confirmed real.

The drug compounds in carfentanil-laced heroin caused massive cerebral infarction, except for areas such as the basal ganglia, which controlled a person's survival instincts, like eating. Since viral encephalopathy was mainly contracted through cannibalism or human-meat consumption, the infected meat could also spread the contagion, causing more and more people to behave like zombies, living dead. The video now showed large throngs of the savages marching down wide boulevards in Russia, Europe, and the United States—footage showing right here in New York City, as well as the border crossing from Mexico, where large crowds of zombies were overwhelming border patrol. Drug users were susceptible, but bite victims were estimated at one-hundred-percent guaranteed infection, Broussard said.

The second-wave pandemic spread through the intake of synthetic carfentanil. Then, it likewise spread through cannibalism after junkies transformed to zombies. Millions of zombie-like savages lurched through the streets on the TV screen, feeding on feeble vagrants who couldn't get up on their feet or couldn't get away after being trapped in side streets, basements, houses.

The carnage wasn't new to me; I stared at the savages with my own yellow eyes, my appearance also transmogrifying, looking just like those monstrous things. These things ate corpse flesh; they could survive by scavenging for meat, even without fresh blood consumption. They were doubly dangerous than meth zombies.

Finally, Broussard issued a dire warning: a cure or vaccine wasn't expected for another two to three years, and the whole world would have to wait until then, when it was probably too late. Sanctuaries were being built on the Appalachians, in remote wilderness areas in Utah and Wyoming. They were erecting concrete walls as high as three floors, preparing for the next generation of survivors. And zombies.

The military was given orders to eradicate the victims.

The rest of the world waited inside the high walls in similar sanctuaries, already decimated from the pandemic. Humankind making its last stand.

"Pray for the world," Broussard said. "Pray for us all. God bless the United States of America," he said before the video went blank.

Static.

THE LAST STAND

Teeth yellow, gums black, limbs scrawny as toothpicks, my hunger pangs intensified. I was going to start feeding for more than survival. Soon.

I abstained from taking more drugs. Rose from my sleeping bag in the sewers, intent on one last mission.

For me, humankind's last stand didn't rest at a sanctuary; it awaited from the frontlines, especially where there were still so many survivors, so many to not give up on.

The hordes of zombies preferred to stay in the sewers during the daytime. They hunted at night, finding a drainage port where they could sneak out in droves and attack people accessible from the streets. Else they fed on corpses, able to live on black blood for weeks.

I was deteriorating. I held onto the walls for support as I planned my next course of action. I had to seal off the zombies somehow. Entomb them alive below, in their home in the sewers. Divert all of the sewage flowing underneath the city to this central zone they inhabited to flush them into the ocean.

City maps would be difficult to procure. But I would find them at the library. So, I traveled across the underground tunnels to reach the New York Public Library and obtain the maps. One cautious step after another proved difficult, my feeble legs barely holding me up. Once I made the decision to do what I could for the remainder of the human race, there was no turning back. I took a hit of meth and my limbs felt exponentially stronger. My eyes saw clearer. I hopped from one set of iron bars in the underground tunnels to another over the raging waters.

I found the drain that opened right below the library and raised it. It was dark up there, and I stripped away some of the shades they had used to cover the windows so I could see. Searching through the periodicals, I finally found a large map rolled up in a cannister inside a box. The label read: *New York City, Underground.* I grabbed it, unrolled the map on a desk.

Tracing the underground tunnels to my location underneath Brooklyn, I searched for the section of the tunnels where the zombies lived. Found it. Then sought for the nearest drainage port the zombies could have been using as an exit point. There was one. Large. Near Central Park, with enough room for hordes to stream out at night. I also traced the waterlines to a network of pipes above that main tunnel. Lady Luck was shining! If I could open that valve or any others in the network of pipes above the tunnel, I could flood enough water from the pipeline to fill the sewer…and drown the zombies.

It was tricky. The only time to do it was during daylight hours, when the zombies retreated below to escape the light.

These zombies were slow. I wasn't supposed to have a problem. Only thing was, I was starting to become a zombie just like them. This meant I wouldn't stand a chance exposing myself to daylight either. I would have to sneak in at dusk just before they ventured out.

I took the map with me when I left the library. Returned to my spot at the sewers to plan my attack. I recorded a video of my last moments as a living human before carrying out my mission.

I placed the smartphone on the ground, camera tilted toward me, and hit record.

"Hello. This is Luzvimindo Arnaiz. You can call me Min, or Mindo. I live here in New York City in the sewers, where I've been staying for the past seven years. I originally migrated from Tondo, Manila, Philippines, one of the first places where the outbreak occurred. My family have long since died.

"I only began taking drugs as a newcomer to New York City, unable to cope with the heartbreak of loss and the difficulty of surviving this way of life after escaping the outbreak years ago. This is me now."

I showed my face to the camera: my gumline, my eyes and my arms and neck, showed the thin strips of meat still hiding beneath the blemished, pierced skin.

"I am transforming. I will not know anything else but hunger soon. I will thirst for blood and crave human flesh. I will commit grisly acts of murder. If you see me, have mercy, kill me and be done with it. Don't let my suffering linger. Put a bullet in my brain. It is an effective means to kill a zombie. A zombie's infected brain is barely functioning. A bullet ends everything. The desire to hunt, feed, and transform others. Everything.

"It is also important that I leave my last suggestion for humankind. I have been outrunning these things for years, and this is what I've observed. The military can follow this example, hunt these things down until the cities are safe again. The zombies live in sewers underneath the city—basically, anywhere light does not shine. Then they go hunt at night, in large numbers.

"In Manila, they live in warehouses, they live in buildings with no access to direct sunlight. In New York City, they're in the subways or in the sewers. If you're in Manila, seal off the buildings so they cannot go out and feed. Starve them. They will die in numbers if they cannot feed on blood and meat. If you live in New York City or other cities in the United States with subways, do as I plan to do. Drown them in the sewers or subways at night. Flood the tunnels all the way to the drainage ports near the ocean. Or seal off these tunnels, the cisterns, or the drainages until they starve.

"It is easier said than done. But if you want to save lives, you better act now before it is too late. Living in the mountains has advantages, but it has disadvantages too. Food is scarce there; so is fresh water. How long will supplies last? The sanctuaries were built to withstand invading armies of zombies, but what if ammunition runs out and the zombies are able to scale the walls? What then?

"It is the last thing I plan to do. For Papa, Mama, and the friends I was not able to save. Farewell."

In tears, I turned off the video, stuffed my phone into my pocket, and set off for Central Park.

When I walked aboveground from the sewer, I hijacked a parked car, dumped my crowbar in the front seat. Keys were hidden in the visor. The oldest gag in the movies also happened often in reality.

I drove quickly under the bleak sky, knowing the zombies were likely to surface at any moment. The drive was only a head start. Traffic was at a standstill up ahead in a major thoroughfare. The drivers had been eaten during the prior outbreak or had escaped in the mad scramble. I abandoned the vehicle and broke into a full run.

The meth was wearing off. I had another hit in my pocket. Careful to not transition fully until the mission was complete, I took the hit and sped up immediately. I ran at what felt like warp speed.

The city was quiet. Most of the survivors were hiding inside the buildings, running out of supplies. Occasional noises rang out. Army trucks were scouring every place, soldiers looking for survivors. People got inside these few trucks, leaving their homes and their slimmer chances behind.

I reached the first foliage and first row of trees in the park, then crossed the meadow full of abandoned tents. There were bodies still there, beginning to rot. The scent drifted in the open breeze like a butcher's shop.

It was easy enough to find the gaping structure—two canals etched in the grassy hill, concrete floors spanning the length of a hundred meters, leading into darkness...and death.

Flashlight in hand, I half-expected to see the things rush out at me. Nothing. I inspected the first batch of pipes on the walls and ceiling and found the first valve nearby. Took my crowbar and jammed the valve, then kicked the crowbar with everything I had. It unlocked only slightly, letting off some water at high pressure. I kept trying, looking into the dark to see whether they were coming. I glanced at the entrance to the tunnel. Dusk was falling.

I kicked the crowbar and it pushed free, so I repeated the process. The valve opened a little more each time, releasing bursts of clean water into the tunnel that poured into the unknown.

One more bit of reworking, and I kicked the crowbar at a really tight juncture. The valve broke. The pipe gave. Water raged down the tunnel from the break in the pipework.

One more break in the pipe and the zombies would be pushed back by the intensity of the flood, trapped inside the main channel to drown, while the rusty iron bars serving as its drainage into the bay would empty the water out. Eventually.

The next job involved shutting down the connecting drainages from the main channel to others like mine, in my area. I knew that I had to close off these other sections and divert flow to the main channel (*Hello, zombies!*) to amass the water all the way to drainage ports into the bay.

I would just need to stand closer to the wall near the broken valve to evade the water from the pipe. If I stood apart from the wall, I'd be in the pathway and in danger of getting attacked by zombies if I lingered too long. These steps needed to be followed in sequence or the zombies would attack me without the rushing water as a line of defense.

Time was ticking.

It wasn't enough to send water down the drainage pipes, as the entire sewer system would take the water in and redistribute it, spilling the water out of the various drainage ports all over the city instead of just the main channel, hence preventing that main channel from flooding. While I trusted the city map, in light of the short time I had taken to review it, I was already beginning to doubt it. But there was no time to doubt. I trusted my instincts, and took my crowbar and unwedged the next valve free. Turned it. It scraped and resisted but, eventually, it turned.

True enough, zombies detected my presence. They appeared out of the darkness at the mouth of the tunnel, clawing at my arms. They thrust their hungry mouths forward and their jaws opened, showing black gums and rotting teeth, a scalloped yellow and green tongue and plenty of festering cold sores and ooze.

I screamed.

They grew in number, lines of them in the tunnel stretching into the heart of never. I pulled my arms away as their long, dead nails tore through the fabric of my shirt, leaving a hole through which deep cuts traced along my skin. I tried to scramble away with everything I had until one zombie with cocoons in her hair lunged forward at my feet. She took a hold of my right shin, keeping me from breaking free.

Death was upon me.

If not the drugs, then the zombies. One of them, a zombie wearing overalls like a city worker, reached forward and gave the death blow. He took a bite out of my forearm as I shielded myself from getting a bite in the neck. I used both hands to push their various faces away, all of whom were successfully taking bites. My skin ripped, dull teeth taking chunks; my bones felt the tips of tongues grazing, tasting, my blood mixing with the blood on the zombies' clothes.

When I fell to the ground, the zombies piled on top. I pushed away frantically, desperate not to be eaten. More bites to my arm, shoulders. More of my screams—like a man tortured. In a flash I saw salvation: the crowbar on the ground at some distance from me. Desperate, I put up one forearm to block the zombies and reached with the other.

I was losing the struggle. The zombie with the cocoons bit my leg. The others began getting through, tearing flesh off my mangled arm. Bone showed through my wrist. My fingers as well. I reached upward with one last gasp of breath and took hold of the crowbar, then began swinging, landing crisp blows to the heads and brains. Their numbers dwindled, but I had to hold my ground.

With mangled arms and hands, I used the crowbar on the zombie with the cocoons in her hair, which scattered across the floor of the tunnel around a puddle of black blood. I scampered to my feet and swung away, cracking skulls and faces, zombies thrown back or pushed to the floor.

I grasped the crowbar tighter, swinging in a wide radius, careful not to lose my weapon. Hatred motivated me as I warded the other zombies off. I remembered Mama and Papa, my friends, eaten. Suddenly, one of the zombies coming toward me looked familiar. It was Melanie, with a zombie baby clinging to her wounded breast by the teeth.

Melanie! Jenny!

Melanie lurched forward and tried to bite me. I got her to back off, swinging the crowbar, warding her away without hitting her, tears welling in my eyes as I gripped the weapon tight. She made one more lunge for my neck before I swung the weapon. Struck her face. Felt my stomach tie in knots.

Spurred by whatever leftover survival instincts I had, I snuck underneath the flood of water pointed at the flailing zombies and used my crowbar to finish the job.

With all my might, I jammed the crowbar in the open break in the pipeline to dislodge the valve completely, sending it ricocheting with a burst of water. All of New York City's water supply began washing down the remaining group of zombies. Down the tunnel, water surged, and in it, bodies whiplashed, submerged.

Entrapping all of their friends in the sewers too.

Including Melanie and Jenny. I watched Melanie flail her arms back under the water pressure and I swallowed hard.

The zombies couldn't get past the high pressure. The entire line from the entrance onward was pushed back, open mouths stuffed with so much liquid their hungry bellies should have burst.

I exited the tunnels and watched all around me for signs of stragglers, grasping my wounds, noticing the black fluid spreading from the bites like a contagion. Lifting my face, I watched the stars twinkling in the sky, realizing I was hearing more and more people emerging from their homes to ride with rescuers. I had bought them just enough time to flee to safety.

When I made my way out of Central Park, I took my smartphone out of my pocket and uploaded the video to the darknet site Mac had previously mentioned—armageddonnet. I hoped that someone would discover my farewell video and have the courage to spread the word.

I returned to the underground tunnels, realizing the massive flood caused by my mission had not been fully contained by the closure of drainage ports. A flood raged down my section of the sewer, not quite as bad as some of the deeper, innermost areas. It was knee-deep at my section, meaning the water filled the tunnel all the way to the ceiling in others.

Still, I found my sleeping bag washed away, my books failing to keep the surge of water from breaking through, pages wading in the dark froth.

I climbed higher to a set of abandoned tunnels untouched by water. Felt weakened by the fading meth in my system, the transformation of cellular nuclei into some form of microorganism, virus.

I awaited my fate.

Below—down below—deep in the cracks of civilization, I laid my bones down to rest at night, where only darkness was a friend.

On starless nights, my bed was cold and grim, wheeling into the heart of darkness—a space in the morgue, a temporary resting place, a prelude to the grave.

Nestled in the cold, I dreamed of childhood's end—the reality that greeted every young man in his rite of passage to adulthood. The coils of heaven. The humus of earth. The inevitable yielding of the body to its pathogen.

Amongst the rodents, the cockroaches, the maggots feeding on my expiring remnants, I made my bed daily, waiting for the tribe of savages, the junkies, the zombies, whatever they were, to take me.

Now that they were gone, I had the entire city to call my own, to roam streets devoid of names and feed on whatsoever I pleased.

Stone on stone, steel beam against steel railing, I've slept in the bosom of darkness, child of the wan in fields of the Nephilim.

My skin was smudged with grime, and sores covered all areas of my body. My eyes were yellow with jaundice. Long, black fingernails caked with filth. My mouth opened into the deep tracts of hell, into a long, silent scream after a lifetime of suffering. My embattled axon and dendron fought against necrosis; amino acids broke down, and fewer blood cells squeezed through increasingly constricted blood vessels.

And my limbs were shriveling. What few muscle fibers remained pulled bones with less dexterity. They were like pulleys, single-mindedly driven by the hunger for blood and meat.

I began forgetting everything. One by one, the memories faded, encephalopathy slowly eating away at each brain cell, eating away at each morsel of memory. There was Papa smiling while helping me learn basic carpentry; Mama hugging me before telling me goodnight; Bodjie, Enrico, Laleng, and Jason's smiling faces, washed away by blood-red eyes; the image of Captain Ruiz on his ship in front of crewmembers, saluting me like I had saved his life and not the other way around. Each memory was replaced by the hunger for flesh, a voracious appetite I needed only sate by climbing aboveground and finding the first susceptible person I see—maybe someone's child, too sick and weak to fight, perhaps a geriatric like Mama and Papa, too old and tired to fend off a rabid teen.

I had become my greatest fear.

I had broken my promise to Mama and Papa.

I was living dead.

I groaned with hunger.

"Aaarrgghh!"

I slept in the mornings and rose in the dark, lumbering, dragging my extremities while grasping at the walls, the scent of carrion entering my nostrils, the scent of fellow humans writhing in the muck, the scent of hubris...

The scent of blood.

My days as a zombie didn't last long. Starved of survivors, I roamed the city for stragglers, finding no new zombies to aid my quest. One dreary day after a long search ended, thankfully, without a successful hunt, I found someone: a military rescuer, patrolling the streets with a rifle in his hand. He signaled to his back-up, telling them he was taking the shot. The tense moment seemed to last forever. The conflict in my muscles propelled me to act. What was left of my mind stirred, starved only of flesh and blood, not love.

Still, destiny was kind.

Mama, Papa... I said somewhere inside of me. *I can be with you now.*

I roared, prepared to attack.

He fired.

And then...

Peace.

THE END

www.ingramcontent.com/pod-product-compliance
Lightning Source LLC
Chambersburg PA
CBHW022139300425
26016CB00006B/181